Danger at Mason's Island
An Angela and Emmie Adventure

Tom Schwarzkopf

NIMBUS
PUBLISHING

Nimbus Publishing Limited
PO Box 9166
Halifax, NS   B3K 5M8
(902) 455-4286

Cover illustration: J.O. Pennanen

Printed and bound in Canada

Library and Archives Canada Cataloguing in Publication

Schwarzkopf, Tom, 1943-
Danger at Mason's Island / Tom Schwarzkopf.
(An Angela and Emmie Adventure)
ISBN 1-55109-562-9

1. Masons Island (N.S.)—Juvenile fiction. 2. Mahone Bay (N.S.)—Juvenile fiction. I. Title. II. Series: Schwarzkopf, Tom, 1943- . Angela and Emmie adventure.

PS8637.C594D35 2006   jC813'.6   C2006-901497-3

Canadä   The Canada Council | Le Conseil des Arts
          for the Arts | du Canada

We acknowledge the financial support of the Government of Canada through the Book Publishing Industry Development Program (BPIDP) and the Canada Council, and of the Province of Nova Scotia through the Department of Tourism, Culture and Heritage for our publishing activities.

*to Emma Jean, with thanks for the
Mason Island stories*

Contents

CHAPTER 1

Summer Hopes Dashed

"Hey Angie, sorry I'm so late." Emmie Seegal bounced up the steps into Angela Black's kitchen and stopped suddenly. Angela was standing there, frozen, with the phone in her hand, and she did not look happy at all.

"That is so unfair," said Angela to herself as she slowly put the phone down.

"What is?" Emmie asked.

"Mrs. Bergen just cancelled."

"What, for next week?"

"No, for the summer. She said thanks for the offer but she'd made other arrangements and wouldn't need us to take care of Colton and Logan."

"But that—that was meant to give us our summer spending money!" Emmie spluttered.

Angela slumped into a kitchen chair, nodding numbly. "I know, I was so looking forward to having that money for clothes and CDs, and…"

Angela was almost in tears as she choked out the last bit. "And maybe if I saved enough, a pair of shoes from William's."

"And don't forget the trip to Wild World Waterpark," Emmie said, joining Angela at the kitchen table and putting her head in her hands. "That was going to be our one big event of the summer."

The two girls sat for a moment in silence. It had been like a dream when Mrs. Bergen asked if they would take care of the twin three-year-olds for the summer. She was going to work at the tourist bureau and the girls were supposed to take the boys to the park, or the wading pool, or for a walk and an ice cream, or whatever. It was the perfect summer job.

And now it had all come crashing down on them.

"Where are we supposed to get a job now that vacation's already started?" Angela broke the silence. "I mean, no one is looking for babysitters now; everyone that needs a sitter has got one lined up."

"Yeah," Emmie agreed, "and what else can we do? We're too young to wait on tables at the café—we can't even wash dishes or work in a store.

Your mom said there was a provincial regulation forbidding hiring anyone under sixteen."

"Well, I'm not waiting until then." Angela shook her long, dark hair angrily. "We'll just have to make our own business."

"Great idea, Angie brain, what should we do?" said Emmie with a touch of sarcasm in her voice. "Set up a lemonade stand on the road?"

"With the little traffic we get down this road, we'd probably go broke and have to drink it all." Angela smiled weakly. "No, there's got to be something we do better than anyone else, or something no one else is doing that needs to be done. My dad calls that finding your niche market."

Emmie sat up. "Niche? Isn't that where an animal lives somewhere exclusive to them and has no competition?"

"Yes, glad you were awake for at least one science class, Miss Emily Louise. But seriously, what are we really, really good at?"

Emmie thought for a long time. "Beside getting into trouble at school?" she finally said. "I don't know."

Before she could think of an answer, Spook the cat stalked in. *Merow?* she asked. *Meerrow?*

"All right," Angela laughed, "I know what you want. Treat time, eh?"

After Spook got her cat treat, Emmie and Angela took a glass of lemonade each, and retired to sit, sip, and think on the wide front porch that looked out over Mahone Bay.

Out on the bay, the sailboats flitted in the sunlight, dodging the big yachts at anchor. Mahone Bay, Nova Scotia, was a favourite tourist spot for boaters and motorists alike, with its wonderful gift and art shops, good restaurants, and neatly kept historic homes and buildings in the town.

Angela's house sat partway up a hill across the bay from the town, and Emmie's farmhouse crowned the same hill. The two homes were a long walk around the hill, down a dusty rural road, and onto the highway—not exactly a pleasant trip. But the girls had discovered a path running up the hill behind Angela's place to Emmie's, through the woods that Angela liked to call the Enchanted Forest, and the girls could visit each other all the time.

Angela thought back to two summers ago, when she moved to Mahone Bay, and, after a long, lonely month alone on this rural road, had met Emmie. Since then, she and Emmie had become the best of friends. The two were inseparable, and except for Emmie's flaming red curls and Angela's coal black hair, they might have been mistaken for twins. Together in school and sports, and always at each other's houses, they had shared many adventures and misadventure. Last summer they had met a retired sea captain who lived on an island in the bay, then saved his life and discovered that he was related to Emmie by marriage. Captain Targus had become a close friend of the family.

But that was last summer, full of adventure and fun. They'd been through a whole year of school since then, looking so forward to this summer. And after they'd lined up the best babysitting job in the world, their plans now lay in ruins. No job, no money, and no prospect of anything but a summer of sheer boredom stretched out before them.

If they wanted trips or shopping, they had to earn their own way, that was very clear. Both sets of parents had firmly told them that at their age, there would be no allowance unless they earned it by doing housework and yardwork over the summer. And any spending money had to either come out of those savings or be earned some other way.

Angela slurped the last of her drink. "Boy, only ten dollars a week for doing dishes and vacuuming and emptying the litter and feeding Spook, and I don't want to even think of what else Mom and Dad have planned for me."

"Me too." Emmie gloomily examined the bottom of her glass. "I've got Bootsie to take care of and the barn cats, and the chickens and…" She got up and stretched. "It's not that I mind doing it."

"Me neither," said Angela as she joined her on the porch step, "it's just that it's not going to be enough. The whole school gang is going to go to Wild World in August, and now we can't go with them. And I saw an adorable top in William's that would go so well with my blue pants, and I wanted to see some movies this summer…" Her voice trailed off.

They both stared off over the bay in silence. They could see their friends' homes, Main Street and William's General Store—bulging, they knew, with summer clothes, CDs, and, of course, the ice cream counter.

But as close as it all was, just across the bay, it might as well have been on the moon, unless they could find some work. Otherwise it was going to be a long, boring, no-money, no-fun summer.

CHAPTER 2
Finding a Niche

"What took you so long?" Angela called from her back porch as Emmie finally emerged from the path in the woods onto Angela's back lawn.

"Sorry," Emmie panted. "I forgot to tell you I had to take care of the Morrisons' animals, and your phone was busy." She dropped down onto the back stoop, sweaty and flushed from racing down the path.

"Oh, Mom was talking to Aunt Laura in England," Angela explained. "Now, what's this about the Morrisons?"

"They've gone up to Halifax for a family get-together and won't be back until Friday, so they asked me again to feed the cats and walk the dog, and Jimmy's got a bunny that has to be fed and watered. And I had to scatter chicken feed in the henhouse and collect all the eggs for the egg man to pick up. I'm exhausted and it's only ten o'clock."

"Do they pay you or is this just being neighbourly?" Angela asked, and then added, "Come on in and get a glass of lemonade."

Emmie got to her feet and followed Angela through the screen door and into the cool of the kitchen. "They offer to pay me every time they go away, and I say no, 'cause they're neighbours, but they always sneak ten or fifteen dollars into my hand when they come back." Emmie drained her glass in one gulp and went over to the sink. "Why do you ask?"

"Because I'm starting to get an idea about how to make some money."

"Oh, no, not another of your money-making ideas," Emmie groaned.

"What's wrong with my ideas? At least I have some!" Angela shot back.

"Well, for one, there was the water thing."

"What? Selling bottled water during the Scarecrow Festival was a great idea, except…"

"Except that Annapolis Springs was a major sponsor of the festival and we were going to sell Creemore Clear."

"How was I supposed to know that? The Annapolis logo was so small on all the advertising; anyone could have missed it." Angela sighed. "You're not the one who had bottled water in her lunch every day right up until Christmas. Anyway this idea is better."

"OK, what is it this time?" Emmie said wearily.

"You've done this animal sitting thing before, right?"

"Lots of times, why?"

Angela ignored the question. "And we have pets of our own that we take care of."

Emmie looked puzzled. "What's your point?"

Angela turned and put her hands on her hips in mock seriousness. "Don't you see? That's our niche."

Emmie looked at her. "Our what?"

"Oh, how soon they forget," Angela teased. "Our niche, our thing that we do that no one else does."

"Oh, that niche. So what?" Emmie rinsed out her glass and put it on the counter.

"So what? That's our ticket to summer fun and funds."

"I'm sorry, I don't see what you're getting at. So I take care of a bunch of animals and we take care of our own pets and…" Emmie stopped in mid sentence. "You mean…"

"Exactly." Angela stood there with a triumphant grin on her face. "Pet sitting! We know cats and dogs—"

"And rabbits, and fish. Don't forget we took care of the aquariums in the ecology room at school all last year." Emmie was getting excited. "And my aunt has lots of birds. I'm sure she'll teach us everything we need to know."

"So what do you think, Emmie?"

Emmie held out her hand. "Shake, partner. E & A Pet Sitting is open for business."

Angela took her hand, then paused and cleared her throat. "I believe 'A' comes before 'E' in the alphabet, and it was my idea."

"A & E it is." Emmie shook her friend's hand. "Now, how do we get customers?"

They both thought about this for a few minutes, then Emmie had an idea. "We could advertise in the *Time 'n Tide* again," she said, referring to the ad that had led to their adventures the previous summer.

"Of course," Angela answered. "Why didn't I think of that?"

"'Cause I'm smarter," Emmie teased. "But it's going to cost us some hard-earned allowance bucks."

"Dad says that if you're trying to start a business, you've got to spend some in order to make some." Angela looked at her friend. "Maybe Mr. Woodward will give us a discount again."

A few hours later, after having hitched a ride into town with Angela's mom, the girls emerged from the *Time 'n Tide* office that was in their English teacher Mr. Woodward's house.

"We're in business!" cried Angela, high-fiving her friend and startling two elderly women who were passing by.

"Right on, partner," said Emmie. "And since you paid for the ad, ice cream at William's is on me."

CHAPTER 3

A Lucky Break

Angela and Emmie sat in the sled at the top of the waterslide, waiting for the attendant to give them the all-clear. A bell rang and Angela braced herself for the wild ride down the flume and into the pool thirty feet below. But nothing happened, except the bell kept ringing and ringing and...

Angela's eyes popped open. The phone beside her bed rang again. Clumsily she groped for the receiver and muttered a sleepy "Hello."

"Well, good morning, young lady," came a cheerful voice from the other end of the line. "I trust I haven't caught you still sleeping at ten o'clock on such a fine day?"

Angela pulled herself into a sitting position and tried to sound wide awake. "Oh no, Captain Targus, I've been up for a while."

"Well that's good, because it's such a wonderful, sunny day, it would be a pity to miss any part of it, wouldn't it?"

Angela wasn't quite as convinced. In fact, since her mom was going to town to work at the library, she had planned today as a sleep-in day. And now she had the Captain—a notorious early bird—cheerfully chatting in her still-asleep ear.

After a few pleasantries, the Captain came to the point. "I was perusing today's copy of the newspaper, and I happened to see your advertisement for pet sitting. What a lucky coincidence, because you two could be the answer to my dilemma."

"What's the problem?" Angela asked anxiously. Was the Captain's cat, Rascal, sick?

"I have to go out of town for a few days, Miss Angela. The company I used to work for, Maritime Ferries, has called me. The mate on a ferry to Newfoundland slipped on deck during a storm and broke both his legs, so he's out of service. They don't have any spare crew right now, so they want me in North Sydney this afternoon to ship out immediately. Good thing I've kept my ticket up to date."

Angela was now sitting bolt upright. "So you would like us to take care of Rascal?"

"Absolutely. Now I'll be docking the *Lady Mary* at the government wharf while I'm away, but

I recall your red-headed friend has a whaler at her disposal for you two to get to the island."

Angela thought for a minute. "Yes, I'm sure Emmie's dad put the boat into the water a few weeks ago and it should be fitted out by now. When do you want us to start? And how long will you be gone?"

"You don't need to come until tomorrow. I'll feed him today and he can have the run of the island. I put a cat flap on the cabin door so he can come and go as he pleases. If you come once a day to feed him and give him a little attention, that'll be perfect. I should only be one or two crossings before they get one of their own back from vacation and onto the vessel, so I figure I'll be home by the weekend. I'll call you when I return, or you'll see the *Lady Mary* gone from the wharf. Is that OK?"

"That's perfect. Rascal will still remember us, and he's so easy to take care of."

"Fine then." The Captain sounded relieved. "Now, what is your rate?"

Angela almost dropped the phone. That was one thing she and Emmie had not even discussed, much less decided. They had completely forgotten to find out what a reasonable charge for their services would be. And here they were with their first customer.

"Well, I'm not sure what's appropriate, seeing as you're a friend and all." Angela stammered while her brain tried to reason.

"Never mind that, now," said the Captain. "I need you and it's worth it for me to know Rascal is in good hands. And as for a special rate for friends, don't do that or you'll be out of business soon, seeing as half the town is your friend one way or the other. No, I'll pay full fare, and you tell me what the tab is when I'm back. You know where Rascal's food is, and the brush?"

"I remember, if it's the same place as last summer."

"Same spot. I'm not one for rearranging things, you know," the Captain laughed. "Well, I'm off to pack. The key is under that log beside the door as always, not that I really need to lock up down here. You just never know, though, if someone from away will come by and decide to explore Mason's Island. Anyway, I must sign off and we'll be talking when I return."

"Goodbye, and thanks." Angela hung up the phone and quickly picked it up again to call Emmie.

A sleepy voice answered. Assuming a cheerful tone, Angela asked, "What are you doing in bed this fine morning, Miss Emily? Why, the sun is shining and the birds are chirping and it would be a shame to lie in bed all day and miss such a wonderful morning."

Her teasing was rewarded with several grumpy swear words, followed by "And what gets *you* up so early, and why are you calling *me*?"

A minute later Emmie was wide awake as Angela told her the good news. "That's terrific," she said. "In fact it's perfect, because it'll give us a recommendation for other prospective customers."

"And what could go wrong?" added Angela. "We know Rascal, we know the island—at least, the part near the Captain's cabin—and it's a short ride in your boat, once a day. But," she continued, "there is just one small detail we forgot."

"What's that?" asked her partner.

"What do we charge?" Angela heard a gasp on the line.

"Oh my gosh, we completely forgot to work that out. What *should* we charge?"

"I don't know. Maybe if we go over to Bridgewater we could go to the mall and ask at Pet Palace."

"Good idea," said Emmie. "We could cut out one of the ads from the paper and ask if they would post it for us. People from Mahone Bay shop there for pet stuff all the time."

"You are so brilliant," Angela replied. "Since we're both up, let's get together and have a late breakfast."

"Or better still," added Emmie, "an early lunch."

"Whatever, I'm on my way. Get decent."

Angela thought for a minute after putting the phone down. Captain Targus was right. It was a wonderful day, and she was going to enjoy it.

CHAPTER 4

Pet Sitting Begins

The sun danced on the wavelets slapping the bottom of Emmie's whaler with a tickety-tickety sound. It was a truly gorgeous day as the girls motored towards Mason's Island. Seagulls wove and dipped in the clear blue sky and cormorants dove deep into the seawater, coming up with a wriggling fish in their beaks.

The two friends sat back in the seats at the front of the boat, letting the salt spray their faces and the wind blow through their hair, marvelling at how good it was to be alive and in business. Today was the first day of pet sitting Captain Targus' cat, and as Mahone Bay shrank behind them and Mason's Island grew larger, they discussed what were reasonable fees to charge for sitting various animals—and what they might do with their earnings.

They passed Lighthouse Island, a low spit of sand stretching out into the channel crowned by a small rise and a white-and-red lighthouse. As was now the case all along the coast, the lighthouse was automatic, even down to the foghorn.

A few minutes later, they reached the large green bulk of Mason's Island and Emmie slowed the boat down, swung parallel to the rocky shore, and headed for the tiny cove where the Captain had his wharf. It looked strangely empty with the *Lady Mary* away in Mahone Bay. The magnificent white-and-brass cruiser was the Captain's pride and joy, and he kept it so neat and clean you could eat off the deck.

They tied up at the dock and walked along the path to the cottage. It was trim and tidy, as was everything the Captain kept. Using the key the Captain had left them, they unlocked the door and were greeted by twelve pounds of excited cat leaping into Angela's arms.

"Whoa, big fellow," she said, as he jumped down and began to circle around his food dish, mewing. "My goodness, he's grown *again* since we were last here!"

Emmie got out the can of cat food from the fridge and spooned a good portion into Rascal's dish. He had acquired his name as a small kitten—one of Emmie's cat's litter—because, though he was the smallest, he was the friskiest and was always getting into trouble. The girls had advertised for a good home for him, and their meeting with Captain Targus had given both Rascal a home and the two girls a new friend.

"Now Rascal," admonished Emmie, "don't eat it all, it has to last for supper too." They changed his water, put out dried food and, holding their noses, cleaned his litter box. After Rascal had eaten and washed up, he pushed open his cat flap, and left for a run.

"We've got some time to stay for a bit," said Angela. "While he's having a prowl, why don't we explore? You know, whenever we come to see Angus, we usually stay near the cabin. I'd love to see the rest of the island. We can take the cellphone with us for safety, though I don't think there's anything bigger than a mouse on this island."

Mason's Island was medium-sized for the area, and mostly overgrown with twenty- to thirty-year-old evergreens and maples. There had been a major fire over the island, and few original trees remained, most of them near the shoreline. A few faint paths ran through the bush, remnants of times when several families lived on the island. There were no traces of the log cabins that had been skidded across the winter ice in the late 1930's, when the Mason clan had moved to the mainland to farm. There was one stone ruin left, however, on a distant corner of the island, its massive chimney visible from the water through the trees.

The warm summer sun flitted through the tree cover, and in the distance they could see it glint on the water. They followed one trail until it ran out, then picked up another. Eventually that trail petered out into scrub brush. Angela looked at her watch.

"We'd better get back and lock up if we're going to get home before supper."

They turned and started back. Suddenly Emmie stopped. "What's that over there?" she asked pointing, then started to walk into the bush.

"I don't think we should go off the track—" Angela started to warn her friend when there was a sudden, terrifying crack of rotted timbers and the ground caved in beneath Emmie's feet.

CHAPTER 5

Rescue and Recovery

Emmie screamed and flung up her hands as she slipped and fell into the hole that had opened up in the ground. Her legs and torso disappeared and only a last-second spreading of her arms over the remaining leaf-covered boards kept her upper body from following. She hung there, suspended over a deep abyss with only the fragile remains of old timbers keeping her from falling deeper. She looked like someone who had fallen through the ice with her arms stretched wide over the rotten boards.

Angela reacted in a flash. She dropped the cellphone and turned toward Emmie. "Don't move!" she ordered. She dropped to her knees and clutched a sturdy tree close to the hole. The ground was solid where she knelt, so she relaxed her grip and untied the jacket she had wound around her waist.

Laying flat on the ground she wiggled as close to the opening as she dared. She crawled up to another sturdy tree growing nearer the edge of the opening and put her arms around it. Then she flung the jacket toward Emmie while hanging onto one of the arms. It landed too far away.

Once again she threw it, and this time it landed close to one of Emmie's arms. "Take hold of the jacket, but move very slowly," Angela told her. Emmie carefully moved her arm and grasped the jacket sleeve. Angela braced herself against the tree and pulled. Emmie didn't budge.

"All right. Hold on tight and slowly bring your other arm over." Angela was thinking fast. Please, she prayed, make this work like the ice-rescue film we saw in gym class.

Emmie slid her other arm slowly over and grabbed the jacket. "Now," instructed Angela, bracing herself even more, "try to pull yourself up and out, hand over hand."

Slowly, agonizingly slowly, Emmie gripped and pulled, gripped and pulled. Pieces of planking broke free and fell into the emptiness below her. They fell for a long time before hitting the bottom with a muffled thud. Angela's arms ached, but she held on. Wedged against the tree, her neck hurt like crazy. Emmie now had most of her upper body free. Carefully she maneuvered herself so she could catch a sapling growing near the hole with one hand. She tested it carefully then pulled on it and the jacket at the same time. With a 'crunch' of broken, rotten wood she came free and rolled onto solid ground.

For a moment both girls lay there, exhausted. A blue jay screamed somewhere in the bush; otherwise it was silent. Then, carefully, they picked themselves up and returned to the path. Angela retrieved the phone and re-tied her jacket around her waist. Emmie brushed off the bits of damp mould and wood clinging to her clothes.

"We'd better get going before someone worries," Emmie said, brushing off the last bits. She turned to Angela. "You really are the best…" she choked up.

Angela threw her arms around her friend. "I couldn't have done anything less, partner." And she smiled as they walked back to the cabin, arms around each other.

The girls agreed that Emmie's brush with danger should be kept secret.

"I feel a bit dishonest not telling our parents," said Angela, "but if they knew, they wouldn't let us go alone to the island again."

"Well if anyone should be punished, it's me," Emmie said as she drew her knees up to her chin. They were sitting in Emmie's bedroom, discussing yesterday's events.

"I wonder what that hole was you fell into," Angela wondered. "It sure seemed deep."

"Probably an old well. Our wells are just small holes, because we've got electric pumps, but the old ones were wide because they were dug by hand and had to be big enough to fit a person."

"How deep do you think it was?"

"Could have been twenty or thirty feet. When you're that close to the sea, you have to go deep to find an underground stream. It could have been full of water, though I didn't hear any splashes when things fell down it." Emmie couldn't help but shiver. "Anyway, from now on we stick to the paths. Do you think it's safe for Rascal with that piece of wood we dragged over it when we went back?"

"I think it should be fine. And I'm glad we swept away the leaves so no one else falls in!" Angela flashed a grin at her friend. She didn't want to admit it, but coming that close to losing her best friend had affected her deeply, and made her realize how close they had become.

They resolved to be much more careful on Mason's Island from now on. Who knew what other legacies were left behind from the families that had lived there?

The most obvious was the old stone ruin. It was perched on a small rise close to the water, screened by a grove of trees at the water's edge. Was it safe enough to explore, as long as they were careful and watched out for any more wells? Perhaps that was something to ask Angus about when he returned.

Three days later Alister phoned Emmie. The town handyman, Alister was also the Captain's friend and a fellow amateur radio operator.

"I've had a call from Angus in St. John's," he said. "He's finished his tour of duty, but is not feeling well and plans to stay a few days longer. He says to just keep on taking care of Rascal until he's back and not to worry."

The next day, when the phone rang, however, Alister sounded graver. "The doctor has checked the Captain into hospital and isn't too sure how long he'll be."

"What's wrong?" Emmie asked.

"I'm not sure, they wouldn't let me talk to him for long, but they said the doctor would contact me as soon as he knew, seeing as me and my wife are just like kin to him, having him over as much as we do. An' you two are like daughters to him, I know that. So as soon as I know what's goin' on, I'll tell you."

Emmie relayed the disturbing information to her friend. "I hope his diabetes isn't troubling him again." Emmie remembered the time last year when they had found the Captain in a diabetic coma.

"I'm sure he's been taking his insulin." Angela tried to be soothing, but she was equally worried about their kind old friend.

They continued their daily trips to the island, but each time they found they had to stay longer to satisfy Rascal's longing for companionship. He often mewed pitifully when they were about to leave, and moped around the cabin. It also seemed to the concerned girls that he wasn't leaving the cabin very often. "I think he's staying inside, waiting for the Captain to return," ventured Angela as they motored back one afternoon. "He looks so sad when we go."

It was several anxious days later when Alister dropped by. "The good news is that Angus is on the mend. An' the bad news is that it's pneumonia, and he'll be in hospital for at least another week before he's strong enough to travel back." That news had Angela and Emmie relieved and worried at the same time.

"Now don't fret too much," continued Alister. "Angus may be getting on a bit, but he's spry and keeps fit. He'll be right as rain in no time. He's more concerned about that cat than he is about himself. Thinks Rascal's goin' ta be lonely without him around. And that kinda worries me. He doesn't need worries like that on his mind when he's supposed to be getting better."

"You tell him we're taking extra time each day to give Rascal some love and affection," said Emmie.

"Right, I will, but you know how he frets over that cat so. I'll try to calm him." And with that Alister got back into his truck and started down the lane back into town.

Angela and Emmie walked slowly back toward Angela's house. They didn't like the idea of their friend sitting in a hospital so far away and worrying about his pet. But what could they do?

CHAPTER 6
Island Sleepover

Early the next morning Angela phoned Alister from Emmie's place. "I have an idea that'll put the Captain's mind at ease. What would you think of us staying on the island until he comes back? To keep Rascal company, I mean. We'd have the cellphone if we need anything, and we'd take sleeping bags and our own groceries."

"Well now, that'd be a great idea. Have you cleared it with your parents? Good, then tell them I can go over with you to make sure everything is shipshape. I'll call Angus and tell him. I'm sure he will be relieved. Give me a call when you're ready to go."

Emmie, who had been listening, glowed with excitement. "Fantastic! We're going to have a giant sleepover on the island!"

"And stay up as late as we want."

"And sleep in as long as we want."

"Or as long as Rascal lets us."

"The island's only about forty minutes from town by boat, and no one'll bother us, 'cause everyone knows it's private property." Emmie started to pull out clothes and stuff them into her bag. "And if we get any other calls for pet sitting, we just motor into town and take care of them."

"I'm glad our parents trust us out there." Angela paused. "But I still feel bad about not telling them about the well."

"That was just stupid of me." Emmie straightened up. "We'll stick to the paths and carry the phone with us everywhere. I should have never gone in for that thing without brushing the leaves away with my foot, one step at a time."

"What thing was it?" Angela slid down off Emmie's bed.

"Something flashing in the leaves." Emmie turned and looked embarrassed. "And you know what it was? The silver paper from a cigarette pack, that's all."

Angela laughed, then she thought for a minute. "That's odd, you know, because the Captain's not a smoker, and neither is Alister, and I don't think anyone else visits him on the island. He usually comes into town to see people."

"Could have blown in on the wind." Emmie bent down and lifted her bag. "Oof, that's heavy."

"I don't think a cigarette paper could blow that far from the mainland. And if it was that shiny, it must have been there fairly recently. I hope no one's trespassing."

Emmie shouldered her bag. "I doubt it. A gull could have picked it up. They'll try to eat anything. Believe me, no one goes over to Mason's Island except the Captain, Alister and us. There's nothing there anyone would want. Now let's get going, Angela Marie."

After Alister had left the island, the girls settled in, spreading their sleeping bags out at one end of the big room in the cabin that served as living room, dining area, and kitchen. They unpacked their groceries and put them away. They were being careful not to abuse their host's food supplies, since they were being paid for sitting Rascal, and felt therefore that they should be responsible for their own meals. Still, it was all right to finish off a half-bottle of pop that was in danger of going flat.

Rascal seemed to sense that the girls were staying, and after eating left for a roam. Angela and Emmie moved outside and set up deck chairs. These were sturdy wooden lounge chairs, the kind that might have been on the passenger decks of the great steamships of yesteryear. They were also immensely more comfortable than any metal and plastic chair. The girls both opened their books, and for a while the only sounds were the occasional buzzing of a fly, or the distant call of a bird. The sun was warm and a little breeze kept it from being beastly hot. Under their hats their eyes grew heavy, the books slowly dropped, and soon each girl had drifted off to sleep in the sun.

When they awoke it was mid-afternoon. The sun had shifted enough that it was no longer directly overhead.

"Do you want to get the boat and do a circle around the island?" Emmie was refreshed from her nap.

"That's a great idea. We haven't seen all of it from the water yet."

Soon they were comfortably seated in the whaler as Emmie slowly motored around the island's rugged coastline. Most of the shore was thickly grown over and the trees clustered right to the edge of the rocky island.

Mason's Island was one of a chain of islands that dotted Mahone Bay, with its seaward coast looking out to far-off Newfoundland. The coastline curved on the near shore and tucked the island in its broad sweep so as to prevent all but the fiercest storms from battering the island. This fortunate geography made it an ideal home for early settlers, but by the 1930s they had all moved to the mainland.

The unbroken ring of trees and rock unfolded before them as they progressed around to the side nearest the mainland. The distant shore facing them was an uninhabited strip that mirrored the wild wooded growth of the island. At the point where the island started to swing away from that lonely stretch of mainland, there was a break in the trees and the looming stone chimney poked its ruined head above the forest crown. The rocks there gave way to a small sand spit, and the remains of a stone jetty poked out at low tide, ending in a tumble of rocks where it buried itself under the waves.

"Man," Angela said. "Except for this and the Captain's cabin, the island is uninhabited. It would be the perfect place for pirates in the olden days, way before the settlers came, don't you think?"

"Could be. Remember, Oak Island and the money pit that's supposedly full of Captain Kidd's treasure is just next bay over from here. Hey, maybe there's buried treasure on Mason's."

"Wouldn't that be cool? Digging up an old chest bound with rotting ropes, and we open it and it's filled with jewels and pearls," Angela said.

"Skip the jewellery. I go for gold coins or gold bars. That would be much easier to covert into clothes and shoes and movies." Emmie steered the boat carefully around the sand bar. "Anyhow, it's not likely to be where that old house was, and if we go looking for treasure, I don't want to find it at the bottom of any wells, thank you."

Angela sighed, then looked at her watch. "We'd better get back and feed Rascal and ourselves. And we promised we'd phone our parents tonight after supper, too."

"Roger." Emmie opened up the motor, and the big boat swung away from the shore, back to the Captain's cove.

"You know," Angela said after a time, "if there were pirates in this area, then there must be stories around about them, right?"

"Huh. Mahone Bay is full of stories, but I don't remember too many about pirates other than the *Teazer*."

She steered the whaler carefully into the little bay. "Still, it might be fun to research it. We've got lots of time on our hands, and it would be a good excuse to go home for a hot tub soak, and then into town."

"Okay, let's go Friday." Angela was getting excited again.

"Deal!" Emmie said as she cut the motor and glided beside the dock.

CHAPTER 7

A Rude Discovery

"Mom, I'm going down to meet Angela and we're going into town to do some resear…I mean, check out some books," Emmie said as she came down the stairs and into the kitchen. The girls had come home to the Bay late that morning to do laundry, have a hot bath, and start their treasure-hunting research.

"OK dear," said Mrs. Seegal, "but do be careful."

"I'm always careful, Mom," Emmie said testily, as she finished towelling her wet hair.

"Uh-huh," her mother replied without looking up from the piecrusts she was rolling. "Like the time you came home in a police car?"

"MOM! Corporal Burrows gave me a lift home 'cause my bike was wrecked."

Her mother straightened up and brushed a wisp of hair away from her face. "And just how did it get wrecked?"

Emmie looked at her feet. "I was swerving to avoid something and didn't see the police car. Anyway it didn't put too big a dent in the door and they didn't make us pay for it."

"Good thing, because you know who would have been paying. Now scoot, and be careful." Mrs. Seegal turned back to her baking while Emmie dumped the towel on a chair and fled out the door.

A few minutes later she stomped out from the path through the Enchanted Forest and on to Angela's lawn, where her chum was waiting.

"Good afternoon Grumpy McGrumpster. Why the scowl?" Angela said cheerily.

"Mom brought up the police car thing again." Emmie grumbled. "Let's get going."

Angela tried to suppress a snicker unsuccessfully.

"Hey," Emmie shot back, "it was all Jeffrey's fault. If he hadn't jumped out from between those cars and scared me, I wouldn't have swerved."

Angela commiserated, "I don't understand what he was trying to do. If he wanted to get your attention, that sure was a funny way of doing it." She sighed. "Boys are so hopelessly immature. And he's such a pain, always bugging you. The only other thing he does is hang around with his cousin Olivia the goody-goody." She put on a squeaky voice. "'Oh dear, I only got ninety-five on that test. I've failed myself.' And she's always rattling on about doing some charity thing, not that there's anything wrong with volunteering, but talking about it all the time? It gets to be just too much. Ugh."

"I certainly hope we don't cross paths with those two this summer," Emmie sighed.

They walked down Indian Road, turned onto the highway and, keeping well to the side, passed the welcoming, open doors of the Mahone Bay Tourist Bureau, and then the famous three churches. Turning toward the centre of town, they soon found themselves in front of William's General Store.

"I vote for a dish of ice cream before we start the research," Emmie said with a grin.

"Unanimous," Angela agreed as they started toward the big glass doors.

"Hey Sunspots, how's it goin'?" someone shouted at them from across the street. Jeffrey Ernst stood there outside the Save-A-Lot with a bag of groceries in his arms, grinning at Emmie, whose face had just turned a vivid shade of red.

"Oh, I am so going to put that twerp in a hospital ward," she said turning to cross the street.

Angela grabbed her arm. "Calm down, he's just trying to get to you. Besides, the last time you smacked him, you wound up in the principal's office."

Emmie stopped, swallowed hard, then relaxed. They turned again toward the store and its ice cream counter. "Anyway," Angela said soothingly, "I think your freckles look really cute." She slowed down. "Oh! I forgot, I've got to pick up Mom's prescription. You go in and order for me; I'll be there in a sec."

She turned and walked briskly toward the pharmacy across the street. Just as she crossed the road, she glanced up the side street at the park and playground, and what she saw made her stop dead in her tracks. She felt her face get red, her blood started to boil, and she nearly pulled an Emmie—she wanted nothing more than to head down the street and put Olivia right next to her cousin, in a hospital bed.

CHAPTER 8

Pirates Ho?

Angela slammed herself onto the stool next to Emmie at William's lunch counter and jabbed her spoon furiously into the waiting dish of vanilla ice cream. Spatters of butterscotch topping flew out onto the counter as she swore through a fake cough.

"What?" Emmie looked up from her ice cream. "Slow down, potty mouth."

"Of all the slimy, foul, scummy things I have ever seen…"

"Whoa. Take a deep breath. What's has got your socks in such a knot?" Emmie swivelled around on the stool to face her red-faced, sputtering friend.

Angela took a deep breath, held it, and let it out slowly. "I was walking over to the pharmacy," she took another breath, "when I saw Olivia at the children's playground."

"No crime in that."

"Wait. She had the Bergen boys with her!"

"What? Was Mrs. Bergen around?"

"No sign of her; in fact, I thought I saw her in the tourist bureau when we passed it. No, that, that…"

"…bottom-feeding scumball stole our babysitting job!" Emmie said it so loud that people in the shoe section looked over at her.

"You two girls OK?" Eleanor asked from her stool at the cash.

"Yeah, we're fine, thanks," Angela managed to blurt out in what she hoped was a normal voice.

"Of all the despicable, dirty…" she said in a low voice.

"Low down, sneaky tricks," finished Emmie. "I'll bet she offered Mrs. Bergen less for one of her than the two of us, even though we would have given the boys much more quality time."

"That was what she wanted when she hired us, two-on-two. I guess we know now what she meant when she said she made other arrangements." Angela stirred the melted puddle of ice cream that was left in her dish aimlessly. All the fire had drained out of her now and her head hung down.

"I wonder how many years you'd get for putting someone in a sack and dropping them off government wharf," Emmie said.

"Probably more than life. Maybe we should just kidnap her and lock her in a root cellar, and then offer to take her place sitting the boys."

"Yeah, there she'd be like Robert Bruce, talking to the spiders and writing poems about mice."

"I think the poetry guy was Robert Burns." Angela sighed. "I'm sure there's a law against kidnapping too. It was so much simpler in the pirate days; grab someone you didn't like, toss them onto a ship, and you had them out of your way."

Emmie laughed. "You probably want flogging brought back, too."

"That might be too gentle for Olivia." Angela stood up and put her tip on the counter. "Anyway, there isn't much we can do about it. Let's get on with our research." She paused. "Hey, we can start right here."

Emmie looked puzzled, then caught on. They moved down the counter, and sat on two stools in front of Eleanor. Angela cleared her throat.

"Well, well, and to what do I owe the pleasure?" Eleanor closed her book, took a quick look to see if anyone else needed anything, and turned her chair to face her two favourite young customers.

"Eleanor," Angela asked, "are there any pirate stories of buried treasure on these islands?"

"Well, they say that all up and down the South Shore in the old days, pirates sailed and hid from the law. You know about the *Teazer*?"

"I know the store in the Bay called the *Teazer*," said Angela, "and I read there about the ghost ship."

"It was a pirate ship—they call it a privateer, but that's just a nice word for pirate. And when they were close to being caught, someone set fire to the gunpowder on board and blew the *Young Teazer* up. Now people here think they see the ghost ship sailing on moonless nights into Mahone Bay."

Emmie broke in. "I know that story, and I know about Oak Island just down the coast, but what about the islands in Mahone Bay?"

Eleanor thought for a moment. "I don't know," she finally said. "Most of them were settled pretty early on by farmers and fishermen, so I don't think there would have been much room for pirates."

"But there's lots of little coves, and some of those islands—like Mason's—are pretty big, aren't they?" Angela was trying to keep up their hopes.

"Well, possibly. I suspect pirates liked their territory uninhabited and real private, and Mason's is way too close to town and the far shore for that. You can see it on a real clear day. Anyway, why are you two so interested in pirates?"

Emmie looked at Angela. Angela paused, then in a burst of inspiration said, "We were trying to get a jump on an assignment for next year's English class. And there might be an essay contest this fall, in the *Time 'n Tide*."

"Well then, you should look in the library." Eleanor smiled, and then in a mock admonishment said, "After all, your mama works there, Angela, and I'm surprised you didn't think of that first."

"Thanks, Eleanor," they chorused, and headed out the door and down the street to the library.

CHAPTER 9

Treasure Hunt

"A-hunting we will go, a-hunting we will go…" Emmie sang as they locked up the cabin door.

"We'll find a little treasure and put it in the bank and we'll spend it all on clothes," Angela finished.

"I wish we had one of those metal detector things," Emmie said as she hoisted the shovel on her shoulder. "It would make this a lot less work."

"Well, we've got at least another week, Alister says. So we can take a path, carefully search that area, and mark it off on this map I started, search another area and another until we strike it rich." Angela grinned at the prospect. "Even if there wasn't anything in those books at the library, I feel treasure in my bones."

"Long as there's no more wells," Emmie said. "I don't want to take that fast a trip downward ever again."

"We'll be vewy, vewy, careful," Angela said in her best Elmer Fudd voice.

They paused for a moment, looking around them at their little bit of paradise. It was another glorious day. The sun dappled through the thick growth of trees, making the day just warm enough, but never too hot. A slight breeze blew over the island and far off they could hear the deep drone of a boat. The cabin stood in a little grove of trees, and it was almost invisible from the cove where their boat rocked at the wharf. The path down to the sea was as neat as any picture in a magazine, right down to the stack of old lobster traps piled by the door, with flowers growing all around them.

Emmie pointed to them. "Do you remember the lobster sandwich story my Gram told us when we were doing the history project?"

"Yeah—that when she lived on the Mahone Bay islands, they were so poor that all they ever had in their lunch was lobster sandwiches?"

"And that they envied the rich kids who had ham in their lunches!"

The girls laughed. "It's hard to feel bad for them," said Angela. "I *wish* my parents could afford lobster for my lunches!"

They walked away from the cottage along one of the more distinct paths, until it branched.

"Robert Frost said to take the road less travelled," Angela said. "I vote for that branch of the trail."

"Works for me; mark it on the map, matey," Emmie said with a pirate's growl. "I think this goes in the general direction of the stone ruin, so I'm not sure it'll be very fruitful."

"Depends on whether pirates camped here before or after the settlers," Angela said, starting down the trail.

"You really are convinced there were pirates on this island, aren't you?"

"And you aren't?" Angela stopped, looking hurt. "You're not just playing along with me, are you?"

"No, not really. I mean, yes, I think there could have been pirates, but they didn't necessarily leave any treasure." Emmie paused. "I think we need to find some sort of mark, like that cross chiseled in the big rock behind your house."

"Oh, please, don't remind me of that fiasco," Angela said. "And that was your idea, anyway, that there was buried treasure under that rock. Man, it took us all week to clean up the mud and the mess from the broken artesian well water pipe, and was my dad ever ticked off."

"I remember only too well," Emmie said. "Listen, I'm with you on this one, but I still think we need some sort of sign to guide us; we can't be digging up the whole island. And when we do find a likely place, we'd better dig nice and neat, and not make a mess. I wouldn't want Angus mad at us."

"Good point on both counts. Let's look for signs first, like crosses or marks on trees."

"Or skulls on poles," Emmie laughed.

They walked on leisurely, scanning each side of the path, looking for clues. Time passed in that dreamy sort of way it does when you are focused on something. In fact, they were so intent on their search that as they rounded a curve in the path, they nearly ran right into The Man.

CHAPTER 10

Intruder Alert

He stood there on the path, seemingly more annoyed than startled at the presence of two young girls. He was big, Angela said afterward, both ways: tall and broad. Not fat, though; he was muscular and tough looking.

He stared at them for what seemed like a full minute, then in an almost angry voice said, "What are you doing here?"

Angela suddenly felt very short, as she craned to look up at him. She felt like she only came up to his big brass belt buckle with the grinning skull on it.

The Man crossed his tattooed arms in front of his striped sailor-like shirt and waited for an answer. Emmie was almost hypnotized by the mass of blue and red snake tattoos that covered his arms and seemed to slither through his thick arm hair.

Angela finally managed to blurt out a reply. "We were out for a walk. Why do you ask?"

The Man stared hard at them. It was then that Angela noticed the angry scar across the left side of his forehead. It ran from just above his eyebrow into the thick, bushy, dark hair on his head, and it seemed to get redder as he spat, "None of your business. You two don't belong down here." He paused and then said carefully, "I would suggest that it would be best for your health to stay away."

Emmie started to say that they had a legitimate reason for being here, and that *he* was the trespasser, but something in his voice made her hesitate. Was he threatening them? It sure sounded like it. And how had he got on to the island?

Angela also considered her reply. Finally she said, "OK. We'll just finish our business here, and stay out of your way."

"What business?" He took a step toward them, then stopped. The girls resisted the instinct to take a backward step, and stood their ground. There was another uncomfortable pause.

"I don't think it's a matter for you to trouble yourself about." Angela wondered how she managed to get that out so calmly. "Come on, Em." She turned and took Emmie's arm. "Let's go."

They walked slowly back up the trail, trying to look calm and cool and casual. Emmie glanced back once. The Man was still standing there, arms crossed, looking hard after them.

Once they were sure he couldn't see them, they broke into a trot. When they reached the main trail, they ran all the way to the cabin, bursting in on a sleeping Rascal and locking the door after them.

Angela collapsed onto her sleeping bag, and tried to catch her breath. Emmie flopped down beside her. "What the heck was that?" she managed to pant out.

"I dunno, but he was a very, very scary dude."

"What right does he have to order us off our—I mean, Angus's island?"

"I wasn't about to argue that point." Angela sat up. "You know, I don't like this one bit, but..." she bit her lip. "If we tell the parents, we'll be so off the island, so quick."

Emmie thought that one through. "You're right. He was scary, but he's obviously not camped on the island. I figure the only way he could've come on is that bit of beach by the ruin."

Their conversation was interrupted by the loud sound of a motorboat—quite near, it seemed, to their part of the island. Carefully, they crept along the floor to the window and peeked over the sill. They could see a slice of the bay through the opening in the trees where their dock was, below. Out in the bay, far enough out that it probably couldn't see their little whaler, a long, sleek, varnished wooden racing boat tore through the water, leaving a huge, rolling wake.

"Wow, what a boat," Angela breathed.

"It's called a cigarette boat," said Emmie. "They're shaped like that for racing, but rum-runners used them in the twenties and thirties. Now they're mostly pleasure boats."

The deep roar of the powerful engine intruded on the silence of the island for another moment, then it was swallowed up by the trees and the sea, and was gone.

CHAPTER 11
False Alarm

Angela and Emmie headed to the police station, where Corporal David Wagner was sitting behind the counter, working on a report. The Mahone Bay detachment was a small operation that had support from Bridgewater whenever needed, but that was rarely necessary—Mahone Bay was a quiet town. Corporal Wagner, and his work partner, Corporal Anne Burrows, liked it here. They knew just about everybody in the town, and were well liked. Sometimes people would drop by just to chat, so Corporal Wagner wasn't surprised when Angela and Emmie banged through the door. He knew the girls well from their participation in school–police activities. They were two of the more eager and vocal participants, and quite likeable, even with their high spirits and overactive imaginations.

"Hello, ladies, and what can we do for you today?"

"Corporal Wagner, just what constitutes trespassing?" Angela asked.

"Why do you ask?"

"Well," Emmie interjected just as Angela was going to reply, "we were over on Mason's Island, taking care of the Captain's cat and all, and there was this guy on the island and he kind of told us to get off and we thought he was trespassing, not us and…"

The Corporal held up his hand. "Whoa. Slow down. I take it you are on the island with the Captain's permission?"

They nodded.

"So you are in the clear. Now, as to anyone else dropping by, as long as no one is doing any harm, or anything illegal, and as long as Angus hasn't ordered them away or posted No Trespassing notices, then there's nothing I can legally do."

"But can he order us off the island?"

"No more than you can unless it's posted. Now the Captain could, but you say he's away?"

Again they nodded.

"I'd guess it's just someone poking around the islands, looking to buy a bit of property, and he doesn't want anyone else to get there first."

"But this guy…I mean, there's no 'for sale' sign or anything, so why…" Angela sputtered.

"Oh, heck," Corporal Wagner said, "there's always people and real estate agents looking for a bit of land anywhere they can. This is one hot place for property—especially islands. Boy, I wish I'd invested when I first got here, I wouldn't be writing out parking tickets now, that's for sure."

The girls looked downcast.

"Sorry," Corporal Wagner said, "no bounty today for turning in an alleged trespasser." He laughed at his little joke. "Now, if he comes back, and I doubt he will, and if you feel comfortable with it, you could ask him politely what his interest is and refer him to Angus when he gets back. OK?"

"OK." Angela and Emmie felt quite small.

"Cheerio then, ladies. I appreciate the concern, but all's square with the law. Have a good day." And he returned to his report as they slowly left the office.

"Well, *that* was a dumb idea," Emmie said when they were well away from the detachment.

"No more dumb than most of yours." Angela bristled.

"I think we're about even on dumb ideas," Emmie said, realizing she had nearly crossed the line.

"So where do we go from here?" Angela said as they continued down Main Street.

"Corporal Wagner doesn't think Scarface is any threat," Emmie replied. "I like that name for him, it's kind of sinister, don't you think?"

"If I remember correctly, it was the nickname for Al Capone."

"Wasn't he the mob guy in Chicago?"

"Yup, but he had connections to Canada. He was into rum-running, I think."

"Well, I don't think our Scarface is a mobster. Not in little old Mahone Bay," Emmie chuckled.

"I don't know. That guy was scary. He looked mean, and he wasn't fooling around when he told us to get off the island." Angela stopped walking while she thought. She kicked a stone idly out of her way.

"He didn't exactly order us off the island; just off that *end* of the island. Anyway, he left in that speedboat, I'm pretty sure, and if the Corporal's right, then we won't see him again."

Angela resumed her walking, head down as she thought. "Maybe, but I think we should just keep to our end for a few days, maybe put the treasure hunting on hold, and just see if he comes back. We'd definitely hear that motorboat."

Emmie nodded. "OK, but that doesn't mean we can't explore closer to the cabin, right? That area wasn't settled in the old days, so maybe it's ripe for the picking."

Angela brightened. "Sounds like a plan, partner. We'll walk quietly and carry a big shovel or something. You're probably right, we won't get any more unwelcome visitors. Now," she looked at her watch, "it's ice cream time. Race you to William's."

CHAPTER 12

Treasure Island

"What do you think of looking for treasure further down the island again?" Emmie was in an adventurous mood. It had been several days since Scarface had been seen on the island, and the idea of any danger had faded, replaced by the excitement of the ongoing treasure hunt.

"If we stick to clear paths and go carefully, it's probably OK," Angela said slowly, still a bit unsure.

"Are you worried about our visitor?"

"No, not really, but I thought we weren't going to go near the ruins."

Emmie paused in her dish-drying. "Well, there's lots of other areas near there we haven't explored, and we'll be able to hear if anyone's there. I'd really like to see it up close, it's got such a spooky feel about it. It's practically begging to be explored."

"I think we got enough ghosts and spooks last summer," Angela said firmly as she hung up her dishtowel. She turned and looked at Emmie, who looked like her bubble had been burst. "Come on, I was teasing," Angela said. "We'll explore the ruins if you really want."

Emmie brightened. "Yay! Get your map and let's go."

For the next hour or so, they poked and prodded patches of sunken ground, oddly shaped mounds, and trees that seemed to have strange marks—all with no results. They paused in their search, resting under one of the few big old trees that had survived the burn over of many years ago. It towered above the rest of the growth, and because of its age they had given the area around it a very careful—yet very fruitless—search.

"I'm starting to think maybe there's no treasure on this old island." Emmie was sweating despite the cool of the forest.

"Maybe." Angela brushed a spiderweb off her shorts. "But it can't hurt to keep looking. We've still got a few more days here, and it's an adventure. Besides," she turned to her friend, "I can't think of a better way of spending the summer than knocking around this beautiful island with my best bud."

Emmie smiled. "Me neither." She stood up and looked around. "Hey, I can see the old ruin. Can we check it out? I'd really like to see it up close."

"I guess it's OK." Angela paused. "Just, let's go slowly and watch out."

They walked softly toward the site, listening carefully for any noise or sign of intrusions. The air was still now, and the woods very quiet. Only the red flash of a cardinal preceded them up the faint, narrow path. Then something up ahead in the bushes rustled.

Angela and Emmie stopped. "Did you hear that?" Angela whispered.

Emmie cocked her head, listening. Finally, she spoke softly. "I thought I heard something, but now it's gone."

They listened for a few minutes more. Silence. Finally they moved on. As they arrived at the scrubby opening that marked the stone foundation, they paused, trying to look through the opening without being seen. For a moment all was still, then there was a crash behind them in the bush.

They jumped and turned, ready to flee, then caught sight of a black squirrel being chased by another, dashing headlong through the leaves and small branches with a sound that was quite out of proportion to its tiny body.

The girls laughed, and turned back to the ruin. As they entered the clearing they saw the edges of what was once a shallow basement, which had over the years filled in. Here and there small saplings grew in the dirt. Nothing else remained of the house except the tops of those fieldstone basement walls and the great fireplace and chimney.

The chimney towered over everything. It had been so well built of fitted and mortared stone that it still stood solid, with only a few stones out of place in its crown. To the two adventurers it looked far more massive than it had from the water.

They wandered carefully around the site, poking through the forest debris with sticks. The wide stone foundation wall ran in front of the chimney, and Angela climbed onto it, then navigated along it until she was standing on the hearth. "Wow, is this ever big," she said, looking up into the stone remains. "I'll bet you could stand up inside the chimney."

"They were made that big so a boy could get in there and clean it. Also for the big cooking pots," said Emmie, proud of her knowledge.

Angela ducked her head inside the great open-ing. She peered upward, letting her eyes adjust to the dim light that came in from the top of the chimney. "Hey, there's a stone shelf inside, just a little way up," she called out.

"It's a smoke shelf. It helped make a draft up the chimney. Sometimes they put a ham on it to smoke it."

"I think I see something up there," Angela called in a muffled voice. She reached up inside the chimney, stretching from her toes. "I can't quite reach it."

She ducked back out of the opening. "Can you give me that stick?"

"Be careful, Angela," Emmie said, passing it to her. Angela ducked back into the chimney. A metal-lic clang came drifting out to where Emmie stood.

"What are you doing?"

"I smacked whatever it was that was shiny, and it's metal," came the echoey reply from inside the fireplace. "Wait, I think I can just get at it with my fingers." A few bits of mortar came tumbling onto the old hearth.

"Angie, watch it. Don't be…" Emmie started to say.

"I've got it," Angela called as she pulled whatever it was down, with a scraping noise. Then she ducked back out of the chimney, and walked carefully along the wall over to where Emmie was standing, carrying a small, plain steel box with a tight-fitting lid. Together they sat down on the rim of the foundation, and looked at it. It was about a foot square and four inches high—like a cookie tin, but with no markings. They tried to pry open the lid. It came off surprisingly easily.

Angela and Emmie stared inside, and gasped in amazement. Then there was a very long silence, for what they saw there absolutely stupefied them.

CHAPTER 13

Mystery and More

"I don't think we should have put it back." Emmie was sitting on her sleeping bag, her book still in her hand. Outside the cabin, an owl hooted. Rascal stirred on Angela's feet, then put his head back down and resumed purring.

"We don't know who put it there or who it belongs to," Angela said firmly.

"No one was here for ages until Angus bought the island. It's probably been up the chimney for years and years. Besides, we were looking for treasure, and we sure found it!"

They both thought back to the incredible sight they had seen in the tin box. There, neatly packed side by side, were about twenty bundles of money, each wrapped in an elastic band and each consisting of about fifty tens or twenties. They guessed that the whole box held between fifteen and twenty thousand dollars! It was a staggering find, one that both thrilled and frightened them. After recovering from their surprise, they had had a long debate about what to do with the money, finally reluctantly returning the box, and its wealth, back to where they had found it.

"Why would anyone stash that much money in an old chimney?" Angela wondered aloud.

"I don't know," said Emmie, crawling into her sleeping bag. "Maybe they felt it was safer than a bank. In the olden days banks sometimes went broke and all the settlers' savings were lost. Maybe when they left the island one of them decided the chimney was a safe hiding place."

She rolled over and pulled her pillow up under her head. "Anyway it's a heap of dough, as my grandpa used to say, and if it doesn't belong to anyone, then it's ours."

Angela turned off the light and lay back. "And what if someone knows it's there and comes for it and finds it gone?" The cabin was silent for a moment as they contemplated this possibility.

"I don't know," said Emmie sleepily. "We'll think about it in the morning."

"All right." Angela turned over in her sleeping bag. Something about that huge stash of money bothered her. It wasn't the money or who it belonged to. There was something else nagging at the corners of her mind, but she couldn't put her finger on it. She closed her eyes and started to drift off.

Angela was just about asleep when it hit her. She sat bolt upright in the sleeping bag. "Emmie, when did you say this island last had settlers?"

"Huh?" answered a sleepy voice.

"When did the Masons leave?"

"Oh for gosh sakes, Angela, I was asleep. I don't remember exactly. Sometime in the 1930s. Why?"

"Who was king then?"

"What on earth has that got to do with any-thing?" Emmie sounded grumpy. "King George the somethingth, I think."

"So money left by the settlers would have his portrait on the bills, right?"

"Yeah, so what?"

"Those bills had Queen Elizabeth on them!"

Emmie sat up. "But…she became queen in 1953!"

"Right, and all Canadian paper money was changed then. Do you see what I'm getting at?"

Emmie was wide awake now. "That money has to be at least newer than 1953."

Angela nodded in the darkness of the cabin. "Not only that, they were all twenties and tens, and those have been redesigned. I've seen the older bills in my Dad's collection, and the ones in that box are what is in circulation today."

"So that money…" Emmie didn't finish her thought, but Angela did.

"Was put there recently. And that means whoever put it there is using the chimney as a safe hiding place and plans to come back for it."

"Maybe we should stake it out and see who comes snooping around. Maybe it's modern day pirates, huh?" Emmie laughed nervously.

Angela lay back down and thought for a minute. "Not pirates, but someone who doesn't want that money to go into a bank for some reason. And probably someone who knows the Captain is away, and hasn't seen our boat yet, and thinks the island is deserted."

"Do you think we should go over to town and tell the police?" Emmie sounded anxious.

"No, what have we got to report? 'There's nothing illegal in hiding money,' that's what Corporal Wagner will say. Still, if we are going to spy, we should be careful, just in case it's got something to do with our nasty visitor. Anyway, that's too much for my tired brain to think about this late, I'm going to sleep."

"Yeah, now that you've got me wide awake," Emmie grumbled. But her only answer was Angela's soft, slow breathing.

The Plot Thickens

"I'm not so sure we should be going back there, Emmie." Angela was clearing up their breakfast dishes while Emmie groomed Rascal.

"Well, how else will we know if anyone claims that money?" Emmie said, emphatically waving the cat brush to make her point. "I mean, the whole point of this pet sitting was to make some money right? If we turn it over to the police and someone claims it, we should get a finder's fee, and with that much dough in the box, we stand to get a nice cut." She finished brushing Rascal, who leapt off her lap and pushed open his cat flap, ready for a ramble. "And, if no one claims it—it's all ours!" Emmie added with a flourish. "So what do you say?"

"Well, OK." Angela sounded less than enthusiastic. "But let's go by land again. It's too easy to be seen from the water. We can take the trail that ends at the rock outcrop behind the ruin. That way we can approach it without being seen. We'd better dress in dark colours so we can't be easily spotted."

"Oh, this is so much fun. It's like some sort of adventure novel, and we are the two heroines out to solve the mystery," Emmie said as she changed quickly into dark pants and top. Angela still wasn't entirely convinced.

They locked up the cabin and started out. As soon as they entered into the bush, they heard the roar of a motorboat nearby. Peeking out from the screen of trees they saw a white powerboat speeding past the island, sweeping up a great wake that came rolling and crashing into the little bay where the whaler was docked.

"Whoever owns that boat ought to slow down near a dockage, but I guess they didn't see our bay from that angle," Emmie said.

They continued their trek through the woods, and soon they reached the branch of the path that led to the back of the ruin. Suddenly they froze. Something that sounded like a scraping noise wafted through the trees.

"What was that?" Angela whispered.

"I don't know. Maybe a crow? They make funny noises sometimes."

They stood in the shadows of the forest for what felt like ages. Nothing stirred. Finally, they moved stealthily, quietly, down the faint path toward the stone rise.

Just as they were about to round the rocky outcrop that hid the ruin from them, they heard something that made them instantly drop to the ground behind the rocks.

"Cal, git the box," a gruff voice called from the other side of the rise.

Another voice grumbled an acknowledgment. The girls stayed still, listening. They were hidden well enough that they were sure they couldn't be seen, but Angela could hear her heart thumping double time.

There was a sound of scraping and grunting, then someone walking on stone. Then he stopped. A squeak told them the tin box was being opened. The gruff voice said, "There you go, my pretties. In with the others. Nice wad, eh?"

"You sure this is safe, Murph?"

"Safe as houses. Who'd think of lookin' here? An' no one sees the transfer, eh? Our man comes tonight and makes the drop, takes his cut, and we got another batch for sale."

They could hear the box being closed and one of the men walking back to the chimney, then the scrape of the box against the smoke shelf. Then there was the sound of something clicking, several times.

The gruff voice called, "Cal, you got a light? My damn lighter's broke." There was a pause, and the sound of two cigarettes being lit and the smoke inhaled.

"Murph, how honest is your man?"

"Well now, you're a fine one to be askin' about honest, aren't you? You ever heard of 'honour among thieves'? Well, he's as honest as we are." The gruff voice, presumably Murph's, let out a laugh. "An' that's why you an' me is comin' here early tonight to hide in them bushes back there. We'll watch him just to make sure he's droppin' off as much as he's being paid fer."

"Ain't that kinda dangerous? What if he's got a gun, or a partner?"

"Nah, he's a loner. Prefers to work that way. Then there's no one to split his take with, eh. And I wouldn't worry about no firearms. He's on probation, and if he's caught with a gun on 'im, it's back to the clink for sure."

Angela and Emmie were cramped and sweating in their hiding place, but they didn't dare move.

The man called Murph continued. "We'd better hide our boat in that bay tonight. No one's around with the Captain fella away so the place is safe."

"What about them two brats that comes to check up on his place?"

Angela and Emmie froze in terror at this mention of themselves, suddenly feeling incredibly exposed and vulnerable. They were sure that they could hear leaves being crunched underfoot. Were the men moving toward them? Could they see them? Angela felt sick!

There was an excruciatingly long silence before Murph spoke.

"Don't think it's a problem. They only comes in the day and goes away quick. But we'll do a quick sweep before we lands, jest to make sure." He laughed coarsely. The leaf-crunching noises stopped.

"What'll you do if we finds 'em?"

"I'll leave that to our boy; he's an expert at arrangin' accidents."

"Accidents?" Cal sounded puzzled.

"Yeah, fallin' down wells or bein' trapped in

burnin' houses—stuff like that." He paused. "What's the matter, Cal, you turnin' yellow on me?"

"No, I ain't afraid. I just don't wanna be part of no…"

"That's why we leaves it to him. He's already got a record."

Angela felt her heart pounding so loud she was sure the men would hear it. Even in the cold of the wet grass she was sweating, and her arm was cramped under her, but she didn't dare move, not even enough to look at Emmie.

There was another excruciatingly long silence on the other side of the rise. Not even a birdcall interrupted the sound of Angela and Emmie's breathing, which Angela was sure the men had heard by now.

Finally Murph said, "Let's get goin' Cal."

They could hear the sound of the men getting up and starting back to their boat.

"Hey!" Murph called suddenly.

The girls' hearts stopped. Had he seen them?

"Pick up yer cigarette butt, Cal. I don't want no trace of us bein' here, OK?"

Emmie and Angela let out the breath they'd been holding. In a moment they heard the scrape

of the boat being pushed off and the motor starting its deep rumble, which increased to a throaty
roar as it started away.

They both stayed down on the damp grass
until the boat could hardly be heard. Eventually,
they got to their feet slowly and shakily. They cau-
tiously looked over the rocky rise to make sure the
men were gone.

Assured they were alone, they turned and, still
shaking in fright, started back to the cabin.

"What do you think that was all about?" asked
Angela when they were well clear of the ruin.

"I don't know. But it sounded like they were
trading cash for—well, for something illegal, I
guess, or they wouldn't be doing it in secret. And
the guy said there would be a drop off tonight."

"Well, at least we know where all that money
comes from."

"From selling whatever it is they've got. They
sound pretty dangerous, Angela." Emmie shivered
at the thought.

Angela paused to catch her breath. "We have
to call the police."

Emmie thought for a minute, then started to
walk again. "No, I don't think we should use the

cellphone. It's too easy for people to overhear calls. But we can take the whaler into town and talk to Corporal Wagner. It's safer that way, and it gets us off this island."

They reached the cabin and unlocked the door. Rascal was waiting for them, and was confused as the girls rushed past him without giving him a pet.

"Did you recognize those guys' voices?" Angela asked as she changed out of her damp clothes.

"Yeah, I think I do. I'm positive the Cal guy is Abe Calloway, a guy from down Overbrooke way. He's a shifty guy that drifts from job to job. I've heard my Dad say he always seems to get into trouble of some sort or other, and then gets let go from whatever work he's doing. I didn't recognize the Murph guy's voice."

They put on their lifejackets as they emerged from the cabin and locked the door, first putting the catch on the cat flap to keep Rascal safe inside. He looked sadly at the girls, but Emmie explained, "It's so you're safe, Rascal. We don't want you wandering around the island with those mean men around. We'll be back tomorrow, so don't you worry."

The sun was bright as they walked down the groomed gravel path to the wharf. *What a day,* thought Angela, now feeling more heroic than she had an hour ago. *So much excitement and adventure.* Her feelings had changed from the terror of being in over their heads to elation at the prospect of becoming a hero for exposing a smuggling ring.

Just ahead, the path curved gently and dropped the last few yards to the dock. The girls rounded the bend, and stopped short as their whole world collapsed. The waves lapped gently against a completely empty wharf. The only sign of the whaler was a bit of rope tied to a post.

CHAPTER 15

Stranded!

They stood there, rooted to the spot, while the realization of what had happened sunk in.

"They took our boat!" Angela cried. "*I know*—they saw us! We heard them talking so they stole our getaway boat!" She sank down on the path and stared at the empty dock.

They both looked out of the bay. Far away they could see Lighthouse Island and beyond it the far shore of the mainland, but there was no sign of the whaler.

Emmie stood there for a moment, then ran down to the wharf. She grabbed the piece of rope in her hands and looked closely at it. "Oh, no. I knew I should have had the painter replaced."

"What…what do you mean?" Angela asked in a daze as she joined her.

Emmie straightened up. "I don't think it was those guys. The rope's not cut, it's frayed, see? It looks like the wash from their powerboat broke the line. It was getting old and I meant to get Alister to splice a new one in when he had the time. And now…" She turned to Angela with tears in her eyes. "I'm going to be in so much trouble when my dad finds out it's gone. What if it washes up on some rocks or sinks? That boat's his pride and joy. Oh, god." She collapsed on the dock, sobbing.

Angela went to put her arms around her friend to comfort her, but she suddenly jerked upright. "Emmie, it's way worse than that. We're stranded here and those thugs are coming back tonight, and we're completely trapped. They said they're going to *look* for us!"

That realization startled the both of them into action. They raced back up the path, unlocked the cabin, and started to look for the cellphone to call for help.

"Here it is," called Emmie pulling it from under a pile of clothes on the floor. She turned it on. A red light glowed ominously, then went out.

"Oh, no." Emmie sounded devastated.

"What's wrong?"

"It's discharged; there's no battery power left. We must have forgotten to charge it after we talked to our parents last night! Oh *no*."

"Try it again," Angela pleaded.

Emmie switched it off, waited, then switched it on again. Nothing happened.

"OK," she muttered, "we just need to find the charger." She started to root around in her pile of clothes on the floor. "I know it's here somewhere." But her frantic burrowing brought no results.

"Let me look," said Angela. She turned every piece of clothing, but no charger.

"Maybe it's in your bag." Emmie's voice was tense.

They emptied both their bags out on the floor, and turned them inside out, scrambling through the mess.

Emmie finally sat up. "It's not here," she said frantically, "It's not on the island. We must have left it on my dresser at home. Angela, what are we going to *do*?"

She brushed away the tears that were starting to form. Rascal rubbed himself against first one set of legs, then another, but no one reached down to pet him. Finally, Angela spoke, trying to sound calm and rational.

"Maybe there's some sort of rowboat or something we can use?"

"Not that I ever saw. Why do you think that?"

"Well—if I remember right, Angus said he used to have to moor the *Lady Mary* offshore and row in before he got the wharf built and the basin dredged. So there must be a boat and a set of oars somewhere, right? Where else would he have left it? Oh, but still, it's such a long way to town, it'll probably take us hours and hours if we can manage it on that open water..." she trailed off, unable to even pretend to be calm.

Emmie had an idea. "If we can find the boat, we could row it over as far as Lighthouse Island, rest there and then row to the shore and hitch a ride into town."

Angela looked doubtful. "Do you think we can row even that far? We're not in the greatest shape."

"It's not really windy and it's better than sitting here waiting for those guys to find us. I mean, we could barricade ourselves in the cabin and lie low and hope they don't find us, but I'd rather not take that chance. I don't want to be stuck in here if Scarface decides to play with matches." She shivered at the thought, even as she tried to make light of it.

"OK. I say we go look for that boat, and if it's seaworthy we go for it. We've still got our life vests on; at least we didn't lose them," said Angela, trying to push the thought of Scarface out of her head.

They searched the cabin, finally finding a pair of old oars under the spare bed, and after grabbing an empty coffee tin for a bailer, went to look for the boat. After much searching, they finally found the rowboat near the path, surrounded by weeds and sapling trees, turned on its back for protection from the elements. They righted it and, panting and puffing, lifted and dragged it to the water's edge. Once in the water it floated, with only a bit of seepage up through the bottom.

"That'll tighten up as we go," said Emmie, getting in. "Come on."

They pushed off and started rowing out of the bay. With one girl on each oar, it went easily for a while. Since it was mid-week, there were only a few boats out of the bay, and those were faint white specks on the horizon.

After a while the slop in the bottom of the boat grew annoying, and Emmie rowed while Angela bailed. They switched places, then switched again. Their shorts were soaked from the water sloshing about in the boat and their knees were sore from having to kneel on the hard bottom to bail.

"I thought you said this would take up," Angela grunted as she threw another can of water over the side. "I swear there's more than ever."

"It's your imagination." Emmie was panting from the exertion. "It always seems like more when you're bailing."

Lighthouse Island grew closer, though not fast enough for the girls. Their backs hurt from the rowing and they were wet and cold. It had been a sunny day, but now the sun was playing peekaboo with the clouds and the air had chilled.

"Emmie, it's definitely leaking more!" Angela was bailing faster now and it seemed that the water was no longer oozing in, it was more like a steady trickle between the floorboards.

"I'm rowing as fast as I can." Sweat poured off Emmie's forehead, and she wondered for a moment how you can be sweating at one end of your body and freezing at the other as her feet sloshed in the cold water.

Now the island was close enough that they could see the dangerous sandbar that it marked, running out to meet them.

"Emmie!" Angela shouted. "It's gushing!"

Emmie stole a glance back to where her friend was bailing frantically. Water poured in the seams of the old boat. There was no time to change places. She rowed twice as fast, with grim determination. Every inch of her arms, shoulders, and back ached like she was on fire.

Angela was flinging water over the stern as fast as she could, but the water level in the boat kept creeping up. Soon it had reached the bottom of the seats. By now they were both wet completely through. The sun had gone behind a big cloud-bank, and the wind had picked up.

Emmie turned the boat straight toward the island and drove it madly on. The oars caught the tips of the waves, drenching the desperate girls even more. Angela was flinging water out so fast that the wind was catching half of it and blowing it back over them.

On they plunged through the rising waves. The water-laden boat was heavier and harder to row now, and the sloshing water was hammering its old boards. They were making little headway. Only the wind seemed to be helping them slightly, as it blew them toward the island.

Then, with a sudden shudder, the bottom of the boat opened up, and within seconds it had sunk under their feet.

For a brief moment of panic the girls found themselves flung into cold seawater, with only their lifejackets to keep them up. But as they let their feet down slowly, they were just able to touch the bottom of the sandbar. With their tired arms propelling them, they were able to reach shallower water, standing firmly on the sandy bottom, and finally stumbling out onto dry land.

A bleak sight greeted them on Lighthouse Island. A long, sandy spit ran out of the sea and up to a small rise where the lighthouse was built. It was a typical red-and-white Maritime structure, rising about thirty feet in the air and surmounted by a glass gallery for the light. A path ran from the beach, up two rotting wooden steps, to the lighthouse door, but the door was locked tight; this was an automated light. Somewhere inside the building a computer controlled when the light came on, and sensed when there was enough fog to sound the foghorn. The rest of the island—all hundred square yards of it—was scrub grass and the occasional rock. The only other feature was a flagpole, faded white, with a frayed rope flapping idly from its top, left over from the days when a lighthouse keeper proudly cared for the light. Even the gulls avoided Lighthouse Island, as there were no mussel beds close by for them to feed on.

The wind continued to whip and chill them. They kept their lifejackets on for a bit of protection, and Angela untied her soggy white school jacket from around her waist and tried to keep it over her shoulders, but they were both chilled.

No one knew where they were, and with the dangerous shoal by the lighthouse, boats gave it a wide berth. There was little chance anyone would pass close enough to see them. The rowboat was wrecked, and they were alone, wet, cold, miserable, and scared.

CHAPTER 16

Old Tales to the Rescue

Angela and Emmie huddled together on the top step of the lighthouse.

"Now what?" Angela wondered aloud. This was far worse than any trouble they had ever gotten into, either in school or at home. The whaler was gone, maybe sunk. They were stranded on an exposed shoal with little hope of rescue, and the smugglers were going to get away. Not that they were her biggest worry right now.

"I don't know." Emmie sounded despondent. In fact, Angela had never seen her friend so low. Usually Angela was the one prone to gloom, and Emmie was the optimist, with her bubbly personality. Now Angela's rock of a friend was just sitting there with her head in her hands, sniffling.

"Is there any way we can signal for help?" Angela was grasping at straws of hope.

"With what?" Emmie snapped. "The air horn is in the boat, and the boat is who knows where."

They lapsed into silence, each wrapped in her own gloomy thoughts. For a moment the sun came out from behind a cloud, but before it could start to warm them it scudded back behind its fluffy covers.

Angela stared out across the water to the faraway green hump that was Mason's Island. Maybe they shouldn't have been so rash and left it. Maybe they could have hidden from the hoods in the woods. After all, it was a big enough island that families had lived there once.

Something about the Mahone Bay islands and settlers skirted the corners of Angela's mind. What was it? Something to do with help? She thought deeply, and finally remembered. The girls had done a history project on settlers' tales this spring, and to help them Emmie's grandmother had told them a story from when her parents lived on the islands in the bay.

"Once when we lived on the island," Gram Wilder had said, "one of the settlers' bulls fell into a well. Now, it was shallow enough that the bull didn't drown, but he was stuck so far down that only his horns were visible over the top. One little lad coming to the well for water saw the horns sticking out and ran for help, shouting, 'the devil is in the well!'

"Now, whenever any islander needed help," Gram Wilder continued, "they would hoist a white bedsheet on a flagpole and the other islanders would come to help out, whether it was as serious as a fire or just the bull stuck in the well. And that's what they did, and eventually got the bull pulled out."

Now, why had she remembered that? Angela sank back into her gloom, then suddenly jumped up.

"That's it!" she cried.

"What is?" said Emmie from between her hands.

"We'll hoist a flag for help, like the settlers did. You remember, your Grandmother told us all about it and we talked about it for our history presentation in front of the class."

"What good is a white flag going to do way out here? And did *you* happen to bring a white bedsheet with you?"

"My school jacket is white. Remember, you teased me about choosing white, because you said it'll always be dirty. Well it's not too grungy, and it needs to dry out anyway. Who knows, maybe someone will see it. Come on, it may be our only hope."

They both got to their feet and walked toward the flagpole. The halyard was fraying and starting to decay, and the wheel at the top of the pole screeched in protest as the girls carefully hauled the white nylon jacket up to the pole's top. The wind caught it and blew it out full, like a flag. Angela prayed that her knots would hold tight. For a long while they stood there, straining their eyes toward Mahone Bay in the hope that a boat, any boat, would come near enough to see the jacket-flag and pull closer for a look.

The sky had been dark since the sun went behind the clouds, but now the sun played around the edges of the cloudbank. Finally it ran out of hiding places and burst out in full glory, illuminating the jacket flapping high up the pole.

"As long as the sun stays out, we might stand a chance of being seen," Emmie said, brightening slightly.

The wait was agonizing. Time crept by. Emmie's watch had stopped, ruined by her dump into the sea, and Angela had left hers back at the cabin.

They didn't even remember what time they had left, only that it had been before lunch, and that just reminded them how hungry they now were.

The afternoon wore on, punctuated only by the sun's frequent departures and reappearances. Nothing moved on the horizon. Time seemed to stop altogether. The girls were slumped on the steps.

"I don't think anyone's gonna ever see that," said Emmie, gesturing toward the jacket on the flagpole. "And anyway, if they do, they won't know it's a signal for help."

"Well, we can't give up hope, can we?" Angela tried to put on a brave face, but deep inside she shared Emmie's pessimism. "Maybe our smugglers will see us and pick us up." She tried to laugh, but when she saw Emmie's face, she apologized. "I'm sorry, Em, I was just joking."

The wind lessened, and with the sun's guest appearances, the friends were starting to dry out a bit. Still, Angela didn't like to think of how miserable it would be if they had to spend the night on this barren sand spit. Nights at Mahone Bay got pleasantly cool if you were sleeping in your own bed, but could be downright chilly if you were outside. And their clothes were still damp from their dunking. There was a danger, she thought, that they could get hypothermia and freeze to death.

She looked out over the horizon. The sun was playing tricks with her eyes, white flashes that looked like a sail were darting in and out of her view. Angela sat up. Was it really the sun on the water? There it was again—no, now it was gone.

"Emmie."

"What?"

"Am I thinking too hard, or is that a sail?"

"Where?"

"Out there." Angela pointed.

They both got to their feet and ran to the top of the hill. Far off, but unmistakable, something like a single sail grew larger on the waves. They strained their eyes in hope.

It truly was a sail and it was headed directly for the island. At once they began to shout and scream. "Over here! Help! Over here!"

The sail grew larger. They could see a black hull now, and two figures crouched in the boat—one handling the sails, the other the tiller.

"Here! Over here! We're stranded! Help!"

A faint voice carried over the waves. "Stand fast, we're coming to get you."

Angela and Emmie hugged each other with joy and ran down the steps to the tiny beach. The small black boat moved closer, its white sails bent to catch the most of the wind. The two figures in it smartly turned it onto another tack. Now they were close enough for the girls to make out who they were.

"It's Jeffrey and Olivia," exclaimed Emmie. "The last two people in the world I expected to see!"

CHAPTER 17

Friends and Salvation

Jeffrey and Olivia! Of all the people in Mahone Bay, what on earth had brought these two misfits to Lighthouse Island?

Emmie ran into the surf and caught the bow of the sailboat. Olivia let the jib sail flap in the wind and Jeffrey brought the large mainsail in tight so the boat stopped.

"Boy, are we glad to see you guys," Emmie said, and she meant every word of it. "What are you doing here?"

Olivia pointed to the flagpole. "Your signal for help," she answered in a matter-of-fact manner.

"Our what?" responded Angela, still in a daze. Was this for real or was she hallucinating? She looked at Emmie, then the boat, and then finally understood. "My jacket!" She ran to untie it from the flagpole, returning to the boat on the run.

"Get in," said Jeffrey. "Emmie, push the bow out into the wind, then hop in and get in the middle with Angela."

Emmie did as directed, and the two cousins set the sails wordlessly and caught the wind. The little boat leapt away from Lighthouse Island. Angela wondered at how smoothly the cousins handled the sailboat. They didn't exchange a word most of the time, adjusting the sails with just a glance at each other. Angela and Emmie huddled up at the bottom of the boat, too cold to speak and still wondering if this salvation was real or just a dream.

Angela finally broke the silence. "Thank you so much for coming to get us."

Jeffrey smiled, and, despite herself, Emmie found herself smiling back. She quickly rearranged her face into a more neutral expression.

"No problem. We were going out for a practice sail anyway."

"Practice?" Emmie didn't understand.

"We're entered in the races in the Boat Festival next month," Olivia explained. "We've been a racing team for...how many years, Jeff?"

"Ever since we were six and your dad built us a little box single-sail boat to putz around in." Jeffrey was keeping a careful eye on their progress as he talked. "We've entered every year in the juniors and won a few."

"A few!" spluttered his cousin, "You've skippered us to a win five years straight." She turned to the girls. "He's so darned modest, I'll bet no one in the school even knows he races."

"WE race!" Jeffrey was insistent. "Just because I skipper doesn't mean you aren't important. You don't really toot your own horn either. Anyway, this year we have to compete in Intermediate against high schoolers, so we've been practicing hard."

"Well," said Emmie slowly, "I must admit I never knew. I mean, I guess I never paid much attention to The Wooden Boat Festival, with us being out of town and all."

"Oh you really should come out," said Jeffrey eagerly, then looked embarrassed.

Olivia looked at her watch. "OK Jeff, we've got just enough time for me to get back and take Colton and Logan."

Emmie shot a dark look at Angela. Angela looked back at her, paused for a moment to collect her thoughts, then chose her words carefully. "Oh, are you taking care of Mrs. Bergen's boys?"

"Just now and then," Olivia said as she adjusted the jib. "She gets called into the tourist bureau once in a while to fill in for people who are on vacation or have to take a sickday." She was still looking at the top of the mast, adjusting the sail as she talked.

Angela cleared her throat. "I thought she was working there full time?"

"It fell through. A bit to port Jeff; the wind's changing."

"Fell through?" Angela was surprised.

Olivia relaxed and turned to her. "Yeah, they had to cut back. They didn't get as much funding from the town as they thought they were going to, so they cancelled her job offer and just use her to fill in. I think it's pretty tough for a single mom to survive on that."

"So you babysit for her when she goes in?" Emmie asked.

"Just watch over them. It's neighbourly."

"Does she pay you?" Emmie was trying to sound nonchalant.

Olivia looked at the sail again and said casually, "Oh, she tries, but I won't take it. They live behind us, right, and she helped nurse my mom when she was really sick, so it's just payback for me."

Angela and Emmie were silently stunned. How could they have got it so wrong?

"Stand by to come about," Jeffrey said to Olivia. "And keep your heads down, you two, or you'll be a lot shorter," he added to his passengers.

"Coming about," he called and shot the boom over Angela's and Emmie's heads as Olivia snapped the jib over to the other side. The little boat turned, caught the wind, and continued its journey on another tack, as they zigzagged closer and closer to Mahone Bay.

Angela swallowed hard. *What an ass I was,* she thought. Maybe Olivia wasn't so bad after all. Maybe she *could* get to like these two classmates, if she got to know them a bit. She also noticed that Emmie kept glancing at Jeffrey. He had filled out a bit, and he was tanned, and she swore he had grown since the last time they saw him.

"Oh, and at the Boat Festival there's street dances every evening," added Olivia. "Last year they got The Purple Slime band in from Halifax for Teen Night, and this year it's Seagull Spit and Friends—they're awesome. And there's a carnival on the Legion grounds and pipers and dancers on the wharf. It's a real party, with people coming from all over the Maritimes. I bought some really neat jewellery there last year."

"In between races," laughed Jeffrey. "Coming about, Liv." And he swung the boom over again.

"OK, I'm convinced," said Emmie. "But, how did you find us and—"

Olivia interrupted her. "Jeff always scans the horizon with binoculars for weather coming into the bay before we go out. He saw something on Lighthouse Island and I went and got Dad's big, high-powered binocs."

"That's when we saw it was a white jacket," added Jeffrey, pulling in the sail a little. "Liv said it was a school jacket. She's got eagle eyes, much better than mine. Then she remembered the project you guys gave in history about the white flags for help and all and concluded that it was you two in trouble—again."

They all laughed, though Angela and Emmie's laughs were more embarrassed than jovial.

"So," continued Jeffrey, "since we had to go for a sail anyway, we decided to investigate."

"And when we heard you holler, we knew we were right," Olivia added.

"Not that it's any of my business," Jeffrey said, glancing sideways at Emmie, "but why were you guys there? It isn't even good for sunbathing."

Emmie looked at Angela, started to speak and then stopped. Angela took over. "We took an old rowboat out for fun, and it sprung a leak and sank. Pretty stupid, eh?"

"Oh, I wouldn't say it's any more stupid than some of the things we've done." Jeffrey pointed the boat to open water between two yachts and trimmed the sail to slow down a bit. "So should we drop you off at your wharf? You look a bit damp, you know."

Emmie started to nod, but Angela interrupted.

"Can you sail all the way into the bay?" Emmie looked at Angela questioningly, but Jeffrey nodded. Angela ignored her. "Then can we go to that little jetty at the head of the bay, just beside the Save-a-Lot. That'll get us right into the centre of town."

"No problem." Jeffrey guided the little sailboat dexterously, weaving around bigger sailboats and motorboats moored in the bay and then setting it in line with the wharf. Emmie was quite amazed at the two sailors' skill. She had never known how manoeuverable a sailboat could be. Perhaps she had been spoiled by motorboats, she thought, and made a note to check out sailing someday.

Within minutes the pair had brought the boat gently alongside the wharf and discharged their passengers. As they clambered out, Angela said, "I don't know how to thank you for rescuing us."

"Thanks is enough," said Jeffrey. "Don't worry about it."

Emmie paused. "Well, how about I treat for ice creams at the Boat Festival? You guys name the date."

"OK," said Olivia. "That'd be nice. Jeff, we'd better get going. Good bye, guys."

And with that they pushed off, swung the boat around to catch the wind and were off.

Emmie looked at Angela. "Why the heck did you get us dropped off here? We look like drowned rats!"

"Never mind that," Angela said. "We don't have much time to get to the police station."

"Hey, I'm not going home in a police car again!" Emmie pulled on Angela's arm.

"Don't worry about that." Angela pulled her arm free and scrambled up the path, with Emmie following reluctantly. "I just hope Corporal Wagner believes us this time."

CHAPTER 18

Stakeout

Corporal Wagner was working quietly at the front desk of the detachment when the two bedraggled girls in salt-stained, damp lifejackets burst into the office.

"Well, ladies, what brings you here today?" he said, putting down the report he had been working on.

"Corporal Wagner. We've caught some smugglers. They're going to meet tonight…"

"Whoa, whoa, slow down. You've done what?"

Emmie took a deep breath. "We've found smugglers using Mason's Island to make their exchange."

"We're not sure what it is they're smuggling, but we overheard them talking," Angela added.

Corporal Wagner leaned back in his chair looking sceptically. "What makes you so sure they're smugglers? This isn't another case of your famous overactive imaginations, is it?"

"No, sir. For one, we found the money they've hidden," said Emmie. "We'd guess it's…how much Angela?"

"Fifteen or twenty thousand dollars!"

Corporal Wagner's chair shot upright as he leaned forward. "Come again?"

"We did a quick count, and there was about twenty thousand dollars in tens and twenties." Angela looked him straight in the eye. "This is no joke, sir. We aren't making it up. We overheard them talking about how they would get the next shipment dropped off tonight, and that they were going to watch to make sure their contact wasn't cheating them."

"They think that with the Captain away the island is deserted, and that we just go there to feed Rascal, that's his cat, but we're staying on the island to keep Rascal company, because the Captain said we could and…" Emmie paused for breath, letting the corporal get a word in.

"You'd better come into the office." He led the way and closed the door, indicating that they should sit down. Then he pulled out his notebook and a pen and settled into a chair behind the desk. "Now," he said, "from the beginning, and go slowly."

They told him everything—or almost everything. They skipped some of the more embarrassing details, like being marooned on Lighthouse Island and their rescue.

"And you think you know one of these guys?"

"I'm almost sure, even though I didn't get a look," Emmie answered. "'Cal' is Abe Calloway's nickname. For a while he was coming to the farm, trying to get my dad to buy firewood, but Dad found out that Cal was cutting it from our own woodlot! Dad chased him off our property with the hatchet, and he left so fast he nearly hit a tree with his truck. I don't think I'll ever forget his whiny voice."

"And the other one was called Murph?" The girls nodded.

Corporal Wagner stroked his chin for a minute then put down his pen. "Now, this might be far-fetched, but did you happen to see if either of them owned an antique wooden racing boat—long and thin?"

"Yes! Oh, what did you call them, Emmie?" Angela said.

"Cigarette boats, my dad calls them."

"Yeah, Scarface had one, but…"

"Scarface?" asked the Corporal, his face getting more serious.

"That's what we call the guy that threatened us on the island."

Corporal Wagner paused for a moment, then said carefully, "Did he have tattoos on his arms?"

"Yes," said Emmie. "Snakes all over them."

"You didn't tell me that before." He sounded slightly angry.

"Well, you said that trespassing wasn't—"

Corporal Wagner cut Angela off. "OK," he said, closing his book. "I think I know what's going on and who's involved. This is getting bigger and nastier than I like." He looked at his watch. "What time did you leave the island?"

The girls looked at each other. "I dunno, maybe ten or so," Emmie guessed.

Corporal Wagner reached into his pocket and produced a twenty dollar bill. He handed it to Angela. "Then I'll guess you're starved. Now get over to Fast Freddy's and get some grub in you. I've got a few calls to make, but I think I'll be needing you, and besides, I want you two to stick close to me. You can freshen up first in our washroom, and leave your lifejackets there."

"Thanks, Corporal Wagner."

"You're welcome. Now listen to me carefully. Don't say a thing when you're in Freddy's. Take a booth at the back and eat your meal, but do not breathe a word of this, it could be…" He searched for words. "It could be dangerous for you if this gets out." He looked at their worried faces, then tried to lighten up with a smile. "Remember, in this town, even the burgers have ears. Try to have fun for half an hour. Oh, and since I'm going to be working through my dinner, please bring me a BLT on brown."

"OK," they chorused, heading for the washroom to clean up.

"And mum's the word." Corporal Wagner walked back out to the front desk, then turned. "Oh, and tell Freddy to go light on the mayo."

A half-hour later to the minute they were back in the Corporal's office. They were surprised to see his partner there too, since the two officers alternated shifts and were rarely on together. Corporal Wagner briefed Corporal Burrows and outlined his plan to the girls.

"So you see," he said, "first we need guides who know that island well. Secondly, there is a requirement for us to be 'called' to the island, and since the Captain is away and you have the responsibility for the property, you will have to see us onto the island. After that, though, I want you two very far away from any action and danger."

The two friends looked at each other in amazement. They were going to be included in a bust—what an adventure this was turning out to be!

Corporal Burrows interrupted. "Now, we need a sketch, as detailed as possible, of the island and all its paths. And put down any old wells or pits you know of—we don't want to be falling in them."

Angela and Emmie shot glances at each other and at the Corporal, but she didn't give any indication that she knew what had happened. Angela nodded. "I can do that, I already mapped the island when we were…"

"Excellent. Now, we've cleared this with your parents," said Corporal Wagner, "providing you do exactly," he looked at them sternly and continued, "*exactly* as we tell you. Understand? It should go smoothly, but there's always the chance that something could go amiss, and I want you two well out of the way and not in the middle of it. Oh, and by the way, Bridgewater told me they have a report of an abandoned boat caught in the marsh down the coast. Miss Seegal, if you'll give me the description of your dad's whaler, I'll check if that's it, and if so ask them to tow it here when they come."

Emmie's eyes brightened, then she paused and said, "You mean, there's more coming?"

"We only have a small launch here, but it's very quiet, so we can sneak up on the island and get ashore. Bridgewater Detachment will bring the big cutter down and move in when the time is right. They're also providing a sergeant who is familiar with the narcotic, tobacco, and alcohol trades. Now you girls will be far away from the action, so no one gets hurt if they decide to put up a fight, though I think both Cal and Murphy are pretty tame. I'm not entirely sure that Scarface, as you call him, won't be packing a gun; he's not really known for sticking to his parole conditions. But after tonight, he won't have to worry about parole!"

Angela and Emmie nodded in assent. The gravity of this adventure had started to sink in, and they were thinking that any slip they made would cancel this once-in-a-lifetime chance to be in on a smuggling raid. If all went well, they could be heroes, and then what would everyone at school think of them? It was almost too exciting to think of.

CHAPTER 19

Silently Through the Night

Dusk was closing in on the sleepy town as the two RCMP officers and their young escorts made their way down the bay, past the government wharf and out along the shore. The police launch puttered along quietly, unnoticed by most of the town; the police had slipped a cover over the RCMP crest on the wheelhouse. Soon they were anchored in a little inlet in line with Lighthouse Island and Mason's Island beyond it. Emmie and Angela watched the cormorants diving for their dinner as the sky darkened over the streaks of a red-and-yellow sunset. Just as visibility was getting down to nothing, they heard the rumble of a large motorboat, and out of the gloom came the Bridgewater police cutter.

It pulled alongside and Emmie was overjoyed to see her whaler swinging from a towrope at its stern. Soon the girls were in the whaler, and had it transferred and fastened to the launch, waiting while the officers exchanged notes and finalized their plans.

Corporal Wagner pulled in their towrope and spoke quietly to them. "Bridgewater has seen Murphy's boat leave, so we're pretty sure they've landed and walked over the island to hide and wait. We'll tow you behind us to the wharf, then you two will take their boat and paddle over to Lighthouse Island and anchor there until I come to get you. Burrows and I will land on the island and go in on the paths, and Bridgewater will go in from the sea to the ruin. As long as our timing works out we should have them, no problem."

He started the launch engine and they moved away at a slow speed, in order to keep the engine as quiet as possible. It was a moonless night, and only the stars illuminated the sea. Out on the water, far away from any lights, the sky was absolutely full of stars, so many that the whole black globe above was like a giant fireworks display.

They slipped into the Captain's bay and approached his wharf. Bobbing gently in the sea was the crooks' white motorboat. There was no sign of its occupants as they cut the launch motor and drifted up to the dock. Corporal Burrows stepped onto the dock and tied up their craft. Then she untied the motorboat and passed the line to Angela.

"Tie it fast," she whispered.

They did as they were instructed and then got out the paddles lashed inside the whaler in case of engine failure. Corporal Wagner untied them from the launch and said in a low voice, "Now, get yourselves over to Lighthouse Island and drop anchor quietly. On no account are you to move until either we or Bridgewater come to get you. Understand?"

Once again the girls nodded. Corporal Wagner let go of the painter, and they started to paddle slowly and as quietly as possible, towing the other craft behind them. Angela glanced over her shoulder at the two RCMP officers standing there in their bulletproof vests. She could see them talking quietly into their radios, each cradling a shotgun over their arm. Yes, she thought, there was no way they wanted to get any closer than Lighthouse Island. The place they wanted to get desperately away from earlier today was suddenly a welcome haven.

It was a harder row than earlier that day. For one, both boats were bigger and heavier. For two, the girls' muscles were sore and achy from the previous row. Also, they were using paddles instead of oars, and that put additional strain on the arms and backs. *On the plus side,* thought Angela, *we don't have to bail and we can go a bit slower.*

They approached Lighthouse Island and carefully skirted the sandbar, anchoring the whaler and the motorboat near the lighthouse. Then they settled in to watch the action. They were ideally located. They could see the edge of the bay that housed the Captain's dock on their left, and on the right, the other side of the island, where the ruin stood. The lighthouse and the rise it stood on shielded them from being seen from any boats approaching from down the coast, which is where the police were certain Scarface would come from.

The boat rocked gently, and a soft breeze wafted overhead. They both had on oversized jackets lent to them by the two police officers and dry lifejackets from the detachment's lockers. A cormorant cried a mournful cry that echoed over the water. They guessed it was close to eleven o'clock by now, and the rocking of their boat lulled them into a drowsy state.

At first it was just a dull murmur that blended in with the sea sounds; then it grew louder. They both sat upright and peered into the darkness. The island blocked their view, but it was definitely a boat coming. Now they could hear it throttling back, then the sound seemed to shift as if the boat were turning. Both girls felt chilled under the big RCMP coats. What if Scarface found them? What if he recognized Murphy's boat? They could be in big trouble. Would the cutter from Bridgewater—somewhere out in the darkness of the far shore—notice and rescue them in time? They held their breath.

The sound of the motor grew fainter, and they started to breathe again. In the starlight they could now see the faint outline of the cigarette boat, with no running lights on, as it headed toward Mason's Island. The stars sparkled on the wake it left behind. The motor sound dropped and the shape of the boat turned inland and was swallowed up by the black blotches of trees along the shore. Silence returned, but now the girls were wide awake, with adrenaline running. Seconds ticked by like hours.

There was a sudden cough of a motor on the far shore, then it sprang into life. In what seemed like seconds, the Bridgewater cutter roared from its hiding place on the shore, crossed the expanse of water between the shore and Lighthouse Island, raced past them like a speeding train and on to Mason's Island. Its lights went on, a huge spotlight shone over the remaining water between the cutter and the shore, and a red light started flashing on the boat, accompanied by a siren.

"Put your hands in the air and don't move." The instructions from a loudspeaker on the cutter carried across the water to the two friends, who were now half-standing in the whaler to get a better view. The whole shoreline by the ruin was lit up with spotlights. They could see figures on the deck of the cutter with shotguns pointed at the shore. Then the cutter dipped behind the screen of trees, and the siren stopped.

Angela and Emmie sank back into the whaler's seats. "Wow," exclaimed Emmie. "I don't think I've ever seen a boat go that fast. That must be one powerful motor in that cutter."

"This is so exciting," said Angela. "Really, how many people can say that they've seen a real smuggling bust, with guns and sirens and everything?"

"I know! This will make the best 'what I did on my summer vacation' essay *ever*."

"And we can tell everyone at the waterpark!"

7   *Danger at Mason's Island*

"YES. Angela, we're like heroes. Finally, we can quit being called the Trouble Twins." Emmie sat back in her seat with a big grin on her face. "I can see the headlines: 'Girls Catch Crooks.' Hey, maybe we'll even get in the Halifax papers. Maybe we'll get on TV!"

They were interrupted by the soft *putt, putt* of the launch with their two RCMP friends aboard. Its running lights gleamed in the darkness as it pulled alongside and cut the motor. Emmie grabbed a line and pulled the whaler in tight to the launch's deck. Corporal Wagner looked pleased.

"Did it go all right?" Angela and Emmie asked together.

"Like clockwork. Your map was excellent. We had them under observation for about an hour before their contact showed up, and that gave us plenty of time to overhear their conversation. Burrows has a complete tape of it. That and the load of American cigarettes in their friend's boat should seal the case. Now you'd better get off to bed, you two. By the way, when did you last feed that cat in the cabin? He was crying at the window when we went by."

"RASCAL!"

"Oh my gosh, we completely forgot about him."

"Poor baby hasn't had anything to eat since breakfast."

"Corporal Wagner, could you take us back to Mason's for a few minutes to feed him, please?" Emmie pleaded.

"Well, we really should seal the island until we've had a chance to go over it in daylight…but I don't see any harm in you feeding that poor animal. What do you say, Burrows?"

"I've got cats myself, so I plead conflict of interest, but as a humanitarian gesture, I'll accompany them on a mission of mercy." Corporal Burrows' eyes sparkled with mischief as she addressed the girls. "Get into the police launch and we'll tow your boat back."

Shortly after midnight, two very tired girls were delivered by police car to their respective homes, stumbled into bed, and immediately fell asleep.

CHAPTER 20

Endings and Beginnings

"So Angel, what exactly were you doing with Corporal Wagner last night?" Angela's mom looked across the breakfast table at her daughter's salt-streaked mat of dark hair as Angela stuffed toast into her mouth.

"Um...I'm not allowed to say," Angela muttered around the crust. And it was true, Corporal Wagner had specifically instructed them not to tell anyone details of what they had seen and heard until the case went to court.

"Not allowed?" Angela's mother sounded skeptical.

"Well, there were some, uh...illegal activities being done at Mason's Island. And Emmie and me found out about it. We helped the police capture the bad guys, but we can't say anything about it until the trial, which won't be for months. And we might be called as witnesses, though Corporal Wagner doesn't want us in public for fear some of the smug…" she caught herself, "some of the crooks' friends, if they've got any, might hassle us."

"Oh dear, I hope that doesn't happen." Mrs. Black sounded worried.

"He said it's just a precaution, because they're small-time crooks and probably won't cause any trouble. But, because it's going to trial, we can't talk about it or we could compromise—that's the word he used—the case." Angela gulped down her milk and pushed her chair away from the table. "Thanks for the late breakfast, mom. I have to wash the sea salt out of my hair, and then Emmie and I need to go to the island, if the Corporal says it's all clear, to feed Rascal."

"Oh, that reminds me," Mrs. Black said, removing the dishes from the table, "Alister called early this morning while you were still deep asleep and asked for you to call him back when you got up."

"I wonder if he has news about Angus? I'll call him right now."

It was good news that greeted Angela when she called. Captain Targus had been released from hospital the night before, and the ferry company was flying him to Halifax, where Alister would meet him and bring him home that day. When Angela got off the phone from Alister, she called Emmie.

"Hullo?" said a sleepy voice on the other end of the line. Emmie brightened up when Angela told her the news, but then Angela had an awful thought.

"Oh my gosh, Emmie, all our stuff is spread everywhere and there's dirty dishes and garbage to take out and—"

"And we've got to clean up the cabin right away!" Emmie said, finishing Angela's thoughts. Angela could hear her jumping out of the bed and rooting around for clothes on her floor as she talked. "I'll call Corporal Wagner and tell him we've just *got* to get on the island. I hope they've finished investigating so we can go to it. He'll probably want to tell Angus what happened, too."

Lucky for the girls, they were docking on Mason's Island an hour later. Soon Rascal was purring contentedly as his friends picked up, cleaned up, and swept the cabin. Then they left a note for Angus, apologizing for sinking his rowboat and promising to tell him everything once Corporal Wagner had briefed him.

"I hope he doesn't think we got into trouble with the police," said Emmie, re-reading the note.

"Add a p.s.," suggested Angela.

"Okay—p.s. We didn't cause any trouble, but the police caught some felons." Emmie spoke as she wrote, pausing to say, "I like that word—felons." She continued writing. "And the police will explain everything to you."

Then Angela added: "p.p.s. Glad you're better, love Angela and Emmie," before giving Rascal one last hug and setting off for home.

It was about two weeks later when they were asked to report to the police station at two o'clock sharp on a Tuesday afternoon. The girls arrived together in Angela's mom's car, a little apprehensive about the reason for their summons. To their surprise, when they walked into the station, Angela's father and Emmie's parents were there, too. Next to them was an older gentleman, with a crown on each of the shoulders of his navy RCMP uniform, and a brown dress belt. Corporals Wagner and Burrows, also dressed in their full serge uniforms, introduced the guest as Inspector Brown from Halifax.

"Ladies," said the Inspector, "I've come down here today to see for myself the fine young people that my staff—" here he paused and indicated the two corporals—"have spoken so highly of. I'm very pleased that you took the initiative to report what you thought might be a crime in progress, and that you were able to assist in the arrest so capably."

He continued. "Now, the matter is still before the courts, so we cannot tell your story outside these walls, but I have briefed your parents and commended them for raising such responsible offspring." He paused to clear his throat.

"Since you cannot get public recognition for what you have done, I have decided to do the next best thing." With that he motioned to Corporals Wagner and Burrows, who each picked up something from the office counter. "We would like to present you with these citations for outstanding contributions to public safety, and welcome you as friends of the RCMP."

With that, the two corporals presented the girls with their framed certificates and the Inspector shook their hands. Then everyone in the room gave them a hearty round of applause. Angela could feel her face flushing red with embarrassment, but she accepted the honour graciously.

"Now," continued Inspector Brown, "I have

one more pleasant duty. The prosecuting attorney has assured me that he will not need to call you two as witnesses, especially since you handed over to us all the money you found. You still mustn't talk about the case, but the Crown has asked me to give each of you a reward for your honesty and your help in solving this case." With that he produced two envelopes and gave one to each of the astonished girls, to more applause from the police officers and the girls' proud parents.

"Wow," said Emmie when she and Angela were back at home. "A hundred dollars each. Even if we do what our parents want and put half of that in the bank, it's still more than enough for the waterpark trip!"

"And with what the Captain paid us, we have spending money for the trip *and* some left over for clothes," Angela added. "I can't belive that this turned out to be such a fabulous summer." She paused, then added, "Oh, by the way, Olivia called last night."

"Oh, really? What did she say?"

"Just invited us to watch the race tomorrow."

"Really? Did she say anything about getting ice cream afterward?" Emmie asked, remembering her offer to treat the cousins.

"I think she was too polite to mention it, but we should take them to William's after the race. What do you say?"

"Sounds good to me." Emmie tried to appear casual, but Angela could see her eyes shining with excitement. She wondered whether it was in anticipation of seeing the race, or seeing one of the racers.

"Oh and one other thing," she said, pausing for effect. "Olivia also wondered if we were going on the water park trip. It seems Jeffrey has been asking about you."

Emmie blushed.

"So, looks like we'll have some company on the trip," Angela said.

Emmie changed the subject quickly. "It's going to be a great finish to this summer. I guess that makes up for not being heroes in the paper and all."

"I suppose," said Angela. "Though that means we'll still be the Trouble Twins next term." She thought back to what had happened over the last few weeks. A job lost; a job found. A treasure hunt with a real treasure, and a real, live smuggling ring! She turned to Emmie.

"I think we've packed far more into this summer than I could have ever imagined. Frankly, I'd like to skip the hero bit. I'm too exhausted. I just hope the rest of the summer vacation is vewy, vewy quiet."

They both laughed, as they started planning the best summer of their lives, all over again.

Don't miss Angela and Emmie's other adventures!

The Ghost at Mahone Bay

Angela and Emmie are looking forward to a vacation before starting Grade Seven. But everywhere they turn, they find another mystery. From strange sounds in the attic to ghostly figures on the shore, things just keep getting weirder. Is there a kind spirit watching over them, like Angela suspects? Or is Angela just too superstitious, like Emmie always says? Either way, these friends definitely have their share of adventure solving the mystery of *The Ghost at Mahone Bay!*

The third book in this series is a Christmas-time adventure! When the town's newspaper editor falls ill, the girls step in to try to save the paper—and Christmas! But have they taken on more than they can handle this time? Find out in Fall 2007!